My Secret Life

What Only I Know
A Mischief Collection of Erotica

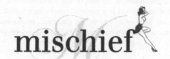

mischief

Mischief
An imprint of HarperCollins*Publishers*
77–85 Fulham Palace Road,
Hammersmith, London W6 8JB

www.mischiefbooks.com

A Paperback Original 2013

First published in Great Britain in ebook format by
HarperCollins*Publishers* 2012

A catalogue record for this book is
available from the British Library

ISBN-13: 9780007534845

Set in Sabon by FMG using Atomic ePublisher from Easypress

Find out more about HarperCollins and the environment at
www.harpercollins.co.uk/green

CONTENTS

Contents

First and Last
Megan Hart

This is the first time.

She wears a dress from her closet, the material smooth and clinging, holding her curves like a lover's hands. It wraps around, ties at the side, dips low in the front. If the wind catches it just right, it'll also show off the black lace garter belt she pulled from her drawer and the span of bare skin at the tops of her sheer stockings. She hopes he'll like what she's wearing, but she dresses for herself. This is how she feels best, sexy underthings beneath a dress any woman might wear. Of course, she's not any woman. She's herself.

She waits without moving, despite the urge to pace. She stands at the window looking out at a parking lot, trees beyond it. Cars pull in and cars pull out. She couldn't tell you the make or model or colour of any one of them. She looks but doesn't see. She waits and waits, every moment tick-tocking through her, while she tries without success to slow the beating of her heart. It throbs in her chest, her throat, her wrists. Between her legs and, just like that, she has to close her eyes and put out a hand to touch the wall and keep herself from falling.

When the door opens behind her, she almost can't look. All of this is real now. Everything they've talked about but never done is going to happen in this room, and she's afraid that when she turns, he won't be the man she's been imagining. That she won't be the woman he's expecting.

If she never opens her eyes, will that make this less real? Or more? There's only one way to find out, and no fear can keep her from wanting to know. She opens her eyes. Turns.

He's smiling, thank God.

'Tess,' he says.

It's not her real name but a secret joke between them. She has blonde hair, blue eyes, fair skin. He says she could be a milkmaid like the one in Thomas Hardy's famous book; sometimes she calls him Angel as part of the game.

It's a little awkward in these first minutes with the door shut and locked behind him and the big bed between them. He doesn't move right away; she's afraid if she takes her hand off the wall she'll have nothing to keep her from going to her knees right there – and there should be something that comes before that. Some dialogue. Some pretence, maybe, that this is something more than what they both know it really is.

Because he doesn't move, she does. One, two, three steps towards him across the soft carpet that threatens to snag the heels of her shoes. She thinks he might say something then, but instead he takes her in his arms and anything that might've been awkward has no chance to grow.

'Hi.' His lips brush the side of her neck.

It's not technically the first time he's touched her, but it lights her up. Sets her on fire. Turns her inside out.

She forgets how to breathe.

His hands settle on her hips and toy with the material of her dress. The hem inches upwards on her thighs. His smile drifts along the slope of her neck to the sweet spot at the curve of her shoulder.

She takes his hand, curls her fingers against his. Moves it over her hip. Slips it inside the slit in her dress, between her legs.

He breathes in when he touches her bare thigh, the top of her stocking, the metal and elastic clip of the garter. When she curls his fingers against her cunt, he breathes out. It's her turn to smile.

He pulls away, just enough to look at her face. When

3

he opens his mouth to speak, she seals off whatever it is he means to say with a kiss. Their first one. Mouths open, tongues stroke, there's the chance their teeth will clash but they don't.

'You taste like chocolate,' she murmurs into his mouth.

Then his fingers shift, and the words are gone. He slides beneath the lace. Finds her clit, the pressure sweet and perfect, just right. She doesn't mean to bite him, but her teeth catch his lip. She mutters an apology but gets out only one syllable before he's kissing her so hard she can't be sure if the blood she tastes is his or her own.

She doesn't care.

His hand is on the back of her head. His mouth on hers. His fingers slide against her, then oh fuck, inside. All the way, thumb still pressing her clit, and she has to grip his shoulder, bury her face in his neck. She bites him again. This time, she means to.

If this had been something sweet and slow, both of them taking their time, something with blowing white curtains and scented candles, music playing in the background, she wouldn't have been surprised. But there's nothing slow about this, and the only music is the sound of his belt unbuckling, the snicker-snack of the zipper going down. The only smells are her perfume and his skin.

Somehow, his shirt is pulled off over his head and tossed aside. His pants go too, kicked off and forgotten as a couple of steps take them to the bed. She's on her back. Mouths fused, he's on top of her for too short a moment until he pushes up onto his knees to undo the tie at her side. He opens her dress, and she watches his face.

He *does* like what she's wearing. He also likes when her back arches, just a little, at the pass of his fingers across the slopes of her breasts exposed by the demi-cup bra. His palms caress her ribs. Her mouth opens. Eyes close.

She wants to touch him. But later. Now, she can think of only being touched.

His hands smooth down, down, over her belly. Her hips, where his fingers squeeze just briefly. When he snaps the lace of her garter belt, she laughs, low. Just a little. Opens her eyes.

He's not looking at her face, so she watches him. How serious his expression as he moves his palms over the outside of her thighs. Then the inside. When his fingertips brush over her panties, the tip of her tongue gets caught tight between her teeth.

'You wear them … over?' Clearly this is not how he ever imagined it to be, the panties worn on top of the garter belt.

So, he's never been with a woman who actually wears such things, or at least never wore them for him. This thought … that she is a first in some way, no matter how small, again punches the breath out of her.

She pushes up on her elbow to hook a finger in the lace, to show him. 'So you can take off the panties without taking off the stockings.'

He blinks. Then again. His lips part and nothing comes out but a wisp of air.

She laughs again. 'You want me to leave the stockings on.'

She didn't ask a question, so he doesn't have to answer. He gives her one with a kiss though, on the softness of her belly. On the jut of her hip bone. His fingers hook into the lace on either side and slide it down as she lifts her hips to make it easy for him.

For the first time since he walked through the door and put his arms around her, she wants to cover herself. Her hands move; she is intimidated and shy and terrified and so turned on she thinks she'll explode.

His hand covers hers. Slides it gently away. She should close her eyes again, in case the truth of how she imagined this doesn't live up to the reality of it, but though she tries to look away, she can't. She doesn't want to see.

She has to.

This is a different kind of kiss, also their first, and softer than the mouth on mouth of earlier. Not hesitant, but gentle. He lingers, the pressure of his lips unbearable until his tongue adds to it and then she understands exactly how much more she can take. Smooth and slow and soft and sweet, that's his tongue against her. The brief press of teeth. The gentle tug of his lips on her clit, and then oh, fuck yes, one finger, then two inside her.

She's been on the edge for days, thinking of this moment. She's been so caught up inside her head that hours have passed without her knowing the full passage of time. She sits down with a book and the pages turn, the chapters end, the book is finished and she can't recall a word of what she's read. People talk to her and she replies without being sure of the question or the answer. The memory of his voice saying her name has made her weak.

And now, all of this is real. It's happening. His mouth is moving on her cunt and she is going up, up and over. She is breaking. Undone. She comes so hard she's not sure if it's a pleasure or a pain, only that sensation slams through her so fiercely she can't do anything but let it hit.

Forever ends, and she looks to find him kneeling between her legs. He's smiling. His hand cups her still-throbbing flesh.

'One,' he says.

She's joked that she'll require at least two, possibly three orgasms before he has one – it's something to aspire to at any rate, though she was only ever half serious. At the moment she's not sure her body could ever possibly rise to climax again, that's how hard the first one hit her. But she's sure willing to try.

She sits. She traces the line of elastic at his waist and admires the bulge of his erection as she cups him through the soft material. 'Take these off.'

He does and kneels again between her legs as she takes his cock in her hand. It's lovely, not that she has a requirement for length or width. When she strokes him, he shivers. She cups his balls while the other hand moves along his shaft, palms the head. He bites his lower lip; it's his turn to close his eyes.

She lies back, her dress still open but not removed, her panties gone but not the stockings. She rubs a satiny foot up his thigh to his belly, then back down. Her legs spread, nothing to hide, he's already had his mouth there after all.

'Fuck me,' she says.

But he doesn't. Instead, he moves his body over hers, his cock thick and hard against her, not inside. She's wet from his mouth and from her orgasm, and his prick slides slippery smooth over her clit. Back and forth. His weight covers her. His mouth finds her neck, kissing. Nibbling. When he pushes up on his arms to keep from crushing her, his cock pushes against her. Always against, not inside, though it would take nothing but a shift of his hips, a tilt of hers, to put him there.

Pleasure builds, slow and steady. She moves with him. Her fingers cup the back of his neck, hold him close as they kiss until, gasping, they need to break for air.

8

Tongues, teeth, lips, he mouths her jaw, her throat, her collarbone. She turns her head to offer her neck, and his teeth leave marks she will only notice later.

There is a point where nothing can stop, no matter what. She's reaching it. His cock on her clit, teasing, teasing, then just the taunting press of the head against her entrance – but he doesn't push inside. He's just getting himself a little wetter so he can slide over her flesh with his and make her crazy. Make her beg for him to fuck her, and she'd do it. She would beg if only she had the voice for words instead of the low and breathless moans.

She uses her hands to speak instead. Nails scratch lightly down his back, anchor at the base of his spine. She pulls him closer and opens herself, tilting her hips so that maybe, just maybe he'll slip inside all the way. Fill her up. And then, before he can, she's coming again in silent, quivering spasms.

'Two,' she hears him say and even in the midst of ecstasy, she's able to laugh.

After that comes a string of words, maybe hers or maybe his. *Fuck me, I want you to fuck me, I want to fuck you, yes, yes, oh, please. Fuck me.*

Fuck me.

I want to fuck you so much. So hard.

Yes. Fuck me hard.

Mindless fuck-talk, it would sound ridiculous if they weren't both naked and sweaty, if he wasn't poised with

9

his cock against her cunt. If he hadn't already made her come on his tongue. But he has, and the words spill out, raw and rough and more honest than anything else they'll probably ever say.

And then at last, he's inside her. All the way. Fills her so deep it almost hurts. And when he moves, oh fuck, oh God, the pleasure doesn't stop, it just keeps going on and on. Her knees press his hips, her feet anchoring at the backs of his thighs. Her hands run up along his smooth chest and discover all his sensitive spots.

It would be OK with her if he let the weight of his body cover her, but he's more of a gentleman than that. He holds himself up to fuck her, at least until she can't stand it any more and pulls him down for another round of kisses that bruise. Bites that sting and send shudders of pleasure through her.

She might be coming again, or she might not have ever stopped. It doesn't matter. They move together just right. Like magic. He's magic for her, and maybe she's a little bit magic for him too.

He's said her name before of course, both the real and the false, but now there's an edge in his tone when he murmurs it. Once, then again. These are not words of love. That's not what this is or what it's meant to be. He says her name as he fucks her because he knows how it makes her feel to hear him say it. Or maybe, she hopes, just a little, he can't keep himself from saying it.

Her name becomes a groan when he comes. His face, pressed to her neck, is hot. Their bodies have become slick with sweat, and her dress has crumpled beneath her. The fabric has bunched and shifted and will leave marks on her skin.

Afterwards they don't sleep, but they do lie side by side in companionable silence while the sweat dries and cools their skin. The sound of the air-conditioning unit kicking on is loud and startling. It turns her head towards him, and she pushes up on one elbow to brush a kiss over his mouth.

She doesn't say she's leaving. She simply gets dressed and goes. In the hall outside the room, she pauses when the door clicks behind her. She turns and puts her hands on it, presses for a moment her cheek against the cool metal, but though she has the key and could open the door, go back inside, get on her knees for him the way she's thought about … she doesn't.

Tess leaves her Angel and goes home to her family, where she wears a different name and is a different woman. Where she cooks and cleans and folds laundry, where she carpools, where she sends spouse and spawn off to work and school every day with a smile so shiny and bright nobody would ever guess what it hides.

***

11

This is the last time.

They meet at his house, a flattering honour she's not sure how to accept gracefully except by agreeing to go. They make small talk in his spotless kitchen. It feels somehow safer and more intimate than meeting in a hotel as they've done every other time. That's why it scares her.

That's why as they face each other from a distance made up of uncertainty and desire, she takes one step, then another, until a third puts her right up close to him. Her hand on his shoulder pushes him back against the marble-topped counter. He's wearing khaki shorts, a white polo shirt. A belt. Nothing wrinkled or rumpled about him. There never is – unless she's had her hands on him the way she does now, tugging his shirt out of his shorts. She slips her hands beneath, palms flat on his belly for a moment before she pulls his shirt off over his head.

Then she goes to her knees.

It's not her natural place, on her knees. Not her usual kink. But for him … she wants to be here. Slowly, her hands travel down his sides, his thighs. Her skirt rides up. Beneath it she wears no stockings. Bare legs. Summer heat makes it too uncomfortable for stockings. The tile floor is hard on her knees. She hopes for bruises to remind her later of what she's done.

Not that she could ever forget. This moment and all

the others have left their imprint on every inch of her. They won't know each other for ever, she knows that much is true. But she'll never forget.

Her hands skate up the backs of his bare calves. She unbuckles and unbuttons him. Unzips. She bares him to her and nuzzles the inside of his thigh while her hand guides his feet out of his shorts and briefs. Details, details. She wants him naked.

Her mouth pressed to the inside of his knee, she looks up. His fingers have curled over the edge of the marble countertop. His mouth is open just a little as he watches her. His cock's already hard. He smiles. She smiles. Her mouth drifts higher, his hair tickling her nose and cheeks and her now-closed eyes. She finds his cock with her mouth and engulfs him.

Her hand on the base, her mouth on the head of his prick, she takes him in as far as she can. Hand meets lips, moving. She sucks a little harder on the head, tongue swirling. She wets him so when her hand strokes the only tug on his flesh is smooth and slick. Good friction. Her other hand cups his balls, thumb stroking backwards to find that lovely pressure point that makes him groan.

Then she slides it between her legs, inside her panties, finds her cunt already wet and slick and hot. Her clit's tight and throbbing under skilled fingers that know just how to move. She could come in half a minute with his cock nudging the back of her throat, but she holds off. Slows down.

She wants all of this to last, even though she knows it's almost over.

She puts his hand into her hair and makes him curl his fingers tight. Makes him pull her hair, just a little, makes him guide her though the truth is she doesn't need him to. She knows where and how to touch him, but making him show her turns her on.

She thinks of herself as a woman, not a lady. Not a girl. But that's what he calls her sometimes, and though she loves it when he says her name in that low voice, edging sharp and hard onto a moan, she also loves it when he calls her his girl. She's not, of course, and never will be. Maybe that's why it hits her so hard in her heart.

This last time, she'd gladly suck him until he comes down her throat, swallow the taste of him, feel him pulse and shudder on her tongue, but he has other ideas. His fingers pull her hair until her face tips up. He's still smiling. He pulls her to her feet – their kisses still haven't become burdened by familiarity. They never will. His hands roam her back, her front, him naked, she clothed. He moves into the family room and the couch.

She's straddling him in a minute, their mouths locked tight, his hands now under her dress. Laughter interrupts their kisses when she shifts and moves to help him get her panties off. When he opens the buttons at the front of her dress and puts his mouth on her breasts, she can no longer laugh. She can barely even sigh, because again she's forgotten how to breathe.

She wants this to last and can't make it. Her body's got an agenda that has nothing to do with what's in her head or heart. She lifts up so he can push inside her all the way, so deep. He fills her. She settles onto him, her forehead to his, her hands cupping his face. Her knees grip his sides and press the back of the couch.

For a long, long moment neither of them moves. Then he murmurs something. Her name, a plea, encouragement. Something low and hoarse and full of need. His voice turns her volcanic. Liquid lava, molten. Her mouth finds his. He whispers into her, breathes for her since she's still unable.

He puts a hand on her hip while the other slides between them to centre on her clit. Just right. Perfect.

They move together at the same time. Time goes thick and slow, a dripping of syrup, of honey. She grips the back of the couch with one hand, his shoulder with the other. They are cheek to cheek, the pleasure too intense for kisses. Fucking's all they can manage. Slow, slow, she moves on his cock, his hand pressing her clit. Her fingers dig deep into his bare skin. Mouth open, her teeth press the side of his neck. When she bites, just a little, he fucks into her hard enough to make her gasp.

I love fucking you.
Yes. Please. Harder. Fuck me.
This feels so good. You feel so good.
Yes. Just like that.

The words come, and she comes with a quiver and a cry, her face pushed against the side of his neck. He knows just how to ease off the pressure on her clit. She pushes herself onto her knees and he keeps moving inside her, not stopping, faster now. And faster. He grips her harder when he comes, his cock so deep inside her they've become one person, just for now. Just this moment, this endless, eternal moment that has become everything. Until there is nothing left.

She cups his face in her hands. She kisses his mouth. They stay locked together for another minute or so, but the moment's passed. She doesn't want to, but she has to move. She has to go. People are waiting for her, and she's lost the ability to hide behind her smile.

He catches her by the wrist just before she steps out the front door. Pulls her back, just one step. 'You can stay. I mean … just for a while.'

She does, for just a while, because although this has ended, she's still not ready for it to be over. If only time was still like syrup she thinks when finally she leaves him with one last kiss. Another hug. No promises of course, that's never been their thing.

That's their goodbye.

It's easy as anything to delete her email address, her instant message account, to unfriend and unfollow and disconnect. To make herself invisible to him. It's so easy it breaks her.

He calls her, once.

She doesn't answer.

And eventually, she remembers how to breathe.

Women's Studies
Kim Dean

'You look tired, Ms Lang. Long night?'

Tressa looked up from her iPad to her driver. As always, Marco's eyes weren't on the road. They were dark in the rear-view mirror and on her. 'Not too bad. I just needed to get ready for this meeting with Professor Walton.'

Marco shook his head. 'You work too hard, boss lady. You should have other things keeping you up at night.'

His gaze flicked down, and she felt it on her thighs where her skirt had ridden too high. She shifted her iPad to cover her bare skin. It didn't matter what the man said to her, there always seemed to be sexual undertones. Still, he was right. She'd worked double-time to get her promotion, but now that she was the first female VP at

18

Catharsis Pharmaceuticals, she had to work even harder to prove she deserved the job. The long hours left little time for things such as a personal life, men, or even flirtation.

'This meeting is important,' she said with a sigh. 'With our budget tightening, I'm trying to determine if we should continue funding the professor's research.'

'What's he study?'

Marco's gaze had slid up to her chest, and Tressa suddenly felt as if the silk tank was cut too low. Her cleavage warmed, and she murmured an answer as she tugged at her suit jacket.

'What was that?'

'*Women.*' She cleared her throat. 'Professor Walton is a leading expert in Women's Studies.'

The grin on Marco's face nearly filled the mirror. 'A man after my own heart.'

'Not like that,' she snapped. 'He's researching the effects of gender and social inequalities on health care.'

As far as she could tell, anyway. It was one reason why she'd taken the time for a personal visit. With as much money as her company had delegated towards the professor's research, she'd been having trouble tracking down the actual study protocols and results.

Marco winked. 'Believe me, beautiful boss. With men, it's always *like that.*' Slowing, he pulled over to the kerb and parked. 'Here we are.'

19

They'd already arrived at the university. Tressa hurried to collect her things but her driver rounded the car before she could exit on her own. He opened the door and took her briefcase. When he extended his other hand, she took it. The clasp was warm and firm, somehow more intimate than a handshake with other men.

The intimacy increased by ten-fold when she stretched her foot to the kerb. The skirt that was already riding too high crept up to her hip. Marco let out a low hum when a sliver of her white panties was exposed. She scrambled out of the car, stood and yanked down the material.

He smiled at her. 'Have a good meeting.'

He tucked her briefcase in her hand and she turned away, feeling far from professional. How did he do that to her? With just a look and a touch? She felt his stare on her ass with every step she took and by the time she made it inside the Women's Studies building, she was a warm, flustered mess.

Smoothing her hair, she searched for her composure before knocking at Office 248.

'Come in.'

She was in control again when she opened the door. 'Dr Walton?'

'Ms Lang.' The professor stood and shook her hand. His touch was firm but cool. He was a thin, erudite man, the opposite of Marco in nearly every way. 'Welcome.

We're excited to have someone from Catharsis visit the lab.'

Her nod was non-committal. He wouldn't be excited if he knew the reason behind her visit. 'I'm interested to see your research.'

'Wonderful.' The professor adjusted his glasses. 'We've been doing some innovative things with the funding your company has provided. So far, the results have been very enlightening. If you'll come this way ...'

Intrigued, she followed as he led her to his lab. Would she finally get some answers? The door was locked. She watched as he put in a complicated code and verified it with a thumbprint sensor. As far as security went, he got top marks. Stepping aside, he let her enter. Tressa looked around with curiosity. The space was cramped. Books and manuals took up one entire wall, while equipment and tools were scattered everywhere else.

'This is an important area of work that has been largely ignored,' the professor said. 'We believe that women will benefit greatly from the results.'

Tressa wasn't familiar with the devices, but she wasn't a physician or a scientist. Her background was in business. 'I'm sorry, but what area would that be?'

The professor's head cocked and his brow furrowed. 'Why, orgasmic manipulation, of course.'

Orgasmic ... The words slowly took meaning in her head, but he couldn't be talking about ...

'Sex toys, Ms Lang. You look surprised.'

Tressa gaped at him. Surprised? She was shocked, to say the least. 'Catharsis funded you to look into issues in women's health care.'

'Yes, that's precisely what we're doing here. Women's sexual health, to be precise.'

Oh, dear Lord. Tressa's fingernails bit into her palms. Marco was right. It was exactly *like that*. She felt blind-sided. Nothing in her preparation for this meeting had indicated this was what was going on at Western University. Had her predecessor known?

She shook her head. 'I'm sorry, Professor, but Catharsis can't support something like this.'

As harmless and scholarly as the professor looked, his eyes went steely. 'Like what? Billions of dollars have been spent studying erectile dysfunction in men. Are you saying, Ms Lang, that women's sexual satisfaction is unimportant?'

'Of course not.' Not when he put it that way.

Walton sighed heavily. 'Ms Lang, I have five graduate assistants relying on that money to get them to their degrees. Five young, brilliant *women*, as a matter of fact. Before you decide to cut our funding, at least take the time to learn more.'

Tressa wasn't sure what she was supposed to do. There was clearly a double standard in play, but where did the ethics stand? He was studying *sex toys*. She needed to talk to the company's lawyers and marketing at the very least, but all that attention would put the spotlight on her. This was not how she wanted to start her career as VP.

Her brain clicked fast. 'Explain to me exactly what the research entails.'

The professor's eyebrows jumped above the rims of his glasses in hope. 'I can do more than explain it to you, I can show you.'

She held up her hand. 'I won't watch something like this.'

'Don't watch. Participate.'

Her mouth dropped open. 'You want to use sex toys on me?'

'How old are you?'

'Thirty-two.' But that was immaterial. It wasn't going to happen. Was it?

'Perfect. I need more data points in that age group. Most of my research subjects are in their early twenties.'

Tressa's weight shifted uncomfortably from one foot to the other. She couldn't actually be considering this – but she was. If the research was on the up and up and she cancelled it, women's groups would surely come after Catharsis. Yet if the studies were strictly prurient, right-leaning political groups would come out with guns blazing. It was a no-win situation for her. 'I suppose I should learn more. Let's just look at our calendars and find a time.'

23

'Let's do it now.'

She stopped short. 'Now? But ...'

'I don't have another class for hours, and I do have the protocol established for my next study.'

'But ...' She couldn't think of a good excuse. She needed to clear up this mess as quickly and quietly as possible, but Marco was right outside, waiting for her.

Marco.

Oh God. Her body began humming again. What would he say if he found out? What would he do if he learned what had happened in here? In the back of her mind, she could hear him daring her. She'd worked for too long. Wasn't it time she got some pleasure in return?

'All right,' she agreed. 'But nobody can know about this.'

'Nobody will. Your identity will be kept confidential.' The professor's shoulders relaxed. Now that he'd been given the chance to fight for his funding, he seemed more at ease. 'I'm sure you'll be happy with your decision. Is there anything in particular that you like? Is there an erogenous zone I should pay special attention to?'

Tressa squirmed. She'd die before she'd tell this analytical geek what got her off. 'Where do we start?'

'You can take off your clothes.' Walton glanced about the room and drummed his fingers against his chin. 'I need to get things ready. I wasn't prepared to run a test case today.'

With that, he left her. Tressa didn't know whether to laugh or be grateful when the studious man practically forgot her. He began puttering around the desk, and she hesitantly reached for her clothes.

The insanity of it all made her numb.

What was she doing? She was the VP for a Fortune 500 company. Had she seriously just volunteered to be a test subject for sex research?

'Modesty is unnecessary.' The professor glanced her way, but then went back to unloading books off a medical table she hadn't noticed before. 'I want you to feel secure and open to new experiences.'

With a deep breath, Tressa took off her suit jacket. The top that she'd thought too low-cut went next, but her hands were sweaty as she reached for the clasp of her bra. The need to hide her nakedness became too strong to ignore. She turned her back on the professor and felt her face heat with embarrassment.

Just get it over with, she told herself. It was too late to back out now.

She yanked on the zipper of her skirt with shaking hands. At last, the only thing holding it up were her clenched fists. Taking a deep breath, she lowered the skirt and stepped out of it.

'The shoes, too,' Walton said. 'It arouses some women to keep them on, but I need you comparable to my control case.'

God, could he be more clinical? Still, it was only that impartiality that allowed her to continue stripping. Soon, she was standing in nothing but her skimpy white panties – the ones Marco had liked so much. She looked down at them.

She simply couldn't.

'Here, let me assist.' The professor was suddenly in front of her. Kneeling, he pulled her underwear down to her ankles.

'Oh!' Tressa gasped. The cool air touched her private parts, and her nakedness was suddenly overwhelming. She couldn't take the intimacy. This man was a stranger and his face was practically in her crotch! She covered her breasts with a forearm as her other hand clamped over the light-coloured curls at the juncture of her legs.

'I need to get some measurements.' Walton walked to his desk and returned with a notebook, a pencil and a tape measure. 'Lift your arms, please.'

Lift her arms? She didn't think so! Remembering the situation, though, forced her to act through her shyness. By fits and starts, she held her arms out to the side. Conflicting emotions ran through her, and she didn't know quite how she felt about this.

'Are your nipples always this turgid?'

He flicked one with his pencil, and she jumped. 'No, not always,' she stammered.

Instinct made her reach for herself again, but Walton

had already wrapped the tape around her and was measuring her bust.

'I'll make a note of it. To ensure consistency, next time I'll have to manipulate them to arousal before I take my measurements.'

Her stomach sucked in hard. Next time? 'This is a one-time deal.'

He looked at her over the top of his glasses. 'Yes, well, one can never tell.'

What did he mean by that?

Tressa yelped when he crouched down in front of her to take another reading. She shifted as embarrassment filled her again, only this time the discomfiture was tinged with arousal.

The tape measure ran directly through her pubic hair, but the professor remained clinical in his evaluation. His nearly stoic behaviour was ironically sensual to her. Her body began to feel almost challenged to gain his attention.

'You have a very nice shape, Ms Lang.' He rolled the tape measure up in his hand. 'You should do well in our experiments. Now, if you'll please move onto the table, feet in the stirrups.'

She eyed the gynaecologist's table with something close to dread, yet Walton seemed immune to her uneasiness as she climbed onto the table. He attached sensors to her chest and neck to monitor her temperature, heart rate and blood pressure. She leaned back but, when he moved to stand between the stirrups, her legs instinctively clamped closed. He waited patiently until she summoned the courage to lift one leg and place her foot in the metal support.

She froze when his gaze went straight to her pussy, but his academic mask was firmly in place. Suddenly, Tressa realised why she was so hesitant. He'd gotten her horny. With all his seeming disinterest and absent-minded touches, he'd aroused her.

It didn't make her feel any better. Now, she was embarrassed that he'd see.

When she didn't move, he caught her other ankle and shifted her into position. Vulnerability made her squeeze her eyes closed. Her pussy was bare and fully visible, but this man wasn't her doctor or her lover.

'Slide down closer to the edge of the table,' he instructed.

The move forced her legs wider open, but even that didn't meet with his approval. He adjusted the stirrups until her knees were spread and her hips were tilted. The position made her defenceless, and her heart began pounding like a big bass drum.

'I need to touch you now,' he said. 'Please relax.'

It was impossible to relax as his hands settled on her inner thighs. Her muscles tightened almost painfully, yet he paid no attention to her resistance. Using his thumbs, he smoothed out the lips of her pussy. 'You're wet. Have you been excited sexually earlier today or are you becoming aroused?'

Her breaths were coming hard. He was looking right into the depths of her, yet Marco unwillingly came to mind. 'Both,' she said in a strained voice.

He slid a finger into her. She was unprepared for the penetration, and the muscles of her lower back contracted reflexively. 'Ooooh,' she moaned as her feet pressed hard against the stirrups.

'That's good.' The professor removed his finger and wiped it on a towel. 'You need to be aroused for the experiment to be effective. It will reduce the amount of lubricant I have to use.'

Tressa's fingers curled into the paper sheet beneath her. Arousal was one thing, but she was fighting to keep it under control. For some reason, she felt she needed to stay at his level, which was purely observatory and analytical.

'I have one more measurement to take before we begin the actual test,' Walton said as he tinkered around his desk. 'I should warn you that you may experience some discomfort.'

Her eyes widened when she saw him pick up a long cylindrical object. 'What is that?'

'I need to measure your vagina. Today's designers have come up with a wide array of orgasmic manipulators, but I wouldn't want to hurt you. The measurements will help me choose the most appropriate device for your pleasure.'

'Oh.' The air seeped out of her lungs. His clinical language reinforced her need to stay controlled, but as she looked at the tool, she didn't know if she could stay objective. 'How does it work?'

He showed her the markings. 'This will measure the length that you are comfortable taking.'

He showed her a switch at the base of the instrument. When pressed, the device expanded. 'Obviously, this will determine the breadth. It can cause some discomfort, but our studies have shown that this can be a key factor for females to achieve orgasm.'

'I understand,' she said inanely. Size mattered.

Once again, the banal little man stepped between her legs. Her hips automatically tilted and he nodded with approval. He tested her wetness with a swipe of his finger and decided to avoid the lubricant entirely. She felt the blunt end of the tool press against her a moment before it was sliding into her.

The hard plastic went up, up, and up. 'Oh! I didn't … *Oooooh!*'

The smooth cylinder was touching her in places that had never been touched. She felt thoroughly impaled, and she squirmed until the professor placed a comforting hand on her tense thigh.

'There are straps overhead if you need something to hold on to.'

Blindly, she reached upwards. Her fingers wrapped around the nylon straps, and the muscles in her arms flexed. With her legs splayed open, there wasn't anywhere she could move. The hardness pushing into her made her want to move, though. Badly.

'A little more ... Yes, there.' Walton leaned down and read the markings on the instrument sticking out of her opening. He picked up his pencil and carefully noted the measurement in his lab book. 'Now this will be a little more intense.'

Tressa's fingers turned white around the straps. God, she wanted to move. The professor, though, was still cool as a cucumber. 'All right,' she said with as much dignity as she could muster.

He flicked the switch, and the effects were devastating. She could feel the pressure increasing. It was as if a man's cock was swelling inside her. Closing her eyes, she let herself enjoy the sensation. Almost immediately, Marco's rugged face appeared.

She whimpered when her mind latched on to the fantasy and wouldn't let go.

'You're doing well.' The professor's hand dropped onto her abdomen. With a firm touch, he tried to calm her.

She was too caught up in the erotic daydream to be soothed. Marco's cock was deep inside her, and it was

31

growing. Her hips surged off the table to take more of him.

'Oh, my!' Professor Walton tried to settle her, but she couldn't stop writhing. Finally, he used his weight to pin her to the table and watched the diameter measurement increase. 'Don't fight it. Let yourself open. Yes, that will do fine.'

'Move it,' she begged. 'Please, do me with it.'

'Now, now. If you orgasm too soon, the experiment will be a failure.'

Tressa groaned as he reversed the motion of the tool and pulled it out of her. She felt empty. She needed something inside her. Her pussy was crying for it. 'Professor, hurry.'

He seemed thrown by the sudden change in her demeanour. Drumming his fingers against his chin, he finally chose a strange-looking item from the nearby table. 'I think this new manipulator will suit you. It's an exciting innovation. The phallic module moves in a lateral fashion, thus simulating the thrusting motion of a man's hips.'

She didn't really care. She just wanted something, *anything* inside her.

'With this option, an added feature is engaged. This doughnut-shaped structure will traverse the length of the phallus, giving added stimulation to the walls of your vagina.'

'Please, Professor.' All her carefully cultivated poise had left her. She was a woman dying to be screwed.

'All right.' The professor frowned as his carefully designed experiment threatened to go awry. 'We'll get started.'

Tressa felt no shyness when he assumed his position between the stirrups. Her hips lifted and her shoulders pressed hard against the table as she waited. The professor didn't waste any time. He'd measured her carefully, and she was displaying all the signs of a woman ready for penetration. He settled the knob of the device against her.

She let out a cry when it slid firmly home.

Walton didn't need any more prompting. He turned on the automated sex toy and watched her reactions closely as the rod pumped in and out of her. 'That's working admirably.'

God, was it! Waves of pleasure coursed through her body. When the shaft lodged deep inside her, she ground her hips into the mattress. In her fantasy, it was Marco fucking her, making her do things they shouldn't.

She jerked, though, when the professor turned on the other feature and that delectable little doughnut began creeping up inside her. The sensation was alarming, and it threw her out of her erotic daydream. She wasn't with Marco. She was on a table in a research lab with her pussy being stretched and invaded.

'Is that stimulus enjoyable?'

She wasn't sure. It felt foreign and unnatural. Sordid. 'Yes,' she groaned.

Her body began thrashing about on the table, and the professor jotted down observations in his notebook as fast as he could write.

'Ahh. I can't ...' Tressa's breath rasped in and out of her lungs. 'Help me.'

The professor frowned. 'You can't climax?' The question prompted his curiosity, and he bent closer to watch the toy fuck her. 'Oh, I see. You have no stimulus on your clitoris.'

His thumb settled against her clit, and her hips surged. Her hands clamped down on the straps, and the stirrups bit into her feet. Electricity swept through her body, and she cried out as she crested. The orgasm held her for a long time. Her body strained to enjoy every last second of it before collapsing onto the table.

Eyes closed, she sank into sated oblivion. Her body lay motionless as the professor removed the toy from her tired pussy.

'That was a most successful case study. I will certainly enjoy analysing the results.'

Tressa flinched when she felt a cool rag settle between her legs, but she was too exhausted to shy away. The professor cleaned the stickiness from her mound and thighs before helping her sit up. 'So what is your conclusion, Ms Lang?'

Her conclusion? God, she couldn't *think*, much less conclude. Her mind was still reeling.

'About the funding.'

Oh, that. The real world came back in bits and pieces until she realised she was a vice president at Catharsis Pharmaceuticals – and she was sitting stark naked in front of a man she didn't even know. She swallowed hard. 'Your funding is secure.'

He was right. Women's sexuality was just as important as men's, and she'd been ignoring her own for too long.

Walton handed her her clothes and she dressed, but he was already entering data into his computer when she slipped on her shoes.

Tressa licked her lips nervously. 'Should I let myself out?'

The professor glanced up and adjusted his glasses on his nose. 'Can I expect you back next week?'

She stopped in her tracks. 'Oh, I don't know. In my position ...'

He looked anxiously at his computer. 'I really need to replicate the results in order for them to have any significance at all.'

Tressa vacillated. 'My schedule is very busy.'

'Twice monthly then.'

She bit her lip. It was tempting to continue. 'You can assure me confidentiality?'

'None of my test subjects has ever been revealed.'

She glanced at the stirrups and felt a tremor run through her. Not even she had been able to find details of these studies, and her never-ending stress had been lifted. She felt relaxed, fulfilled, and sexy as hell.

Marco would never know the better.

That sealed the deal. 'Have the confidentiality agreement written up. I'll be here the second and fourth Wednesdays of the month.'

Walton smiled. 'Your data could mean the difference to countless women struggling with frigidity.'

And it would mean the difference to her in a life that had become too intent on work and so devoid of pleasure. A secret little interlude. Tressa smiled softly. She couldn't risk her job by having an affair with her driver – not yet – but she could be a test subject for one of the country's leading sex researchers.

She just had to make sure Marco drove her every week.

Mr Wrong
Justine Elyot

He's a dangerous person. He's bad for me. Everybody hates him. He's arrogant and faithless, self-absorbed and cruel.

When he dumped me, three years ago, by publicly feeling up another woman at my twenty-fifth birthday party, all my friends practically haemorrhaged with relief.

'I didn't like to say anything at the time but …'

'I know you were really loved-up but …'

'I was dreading the wedding invitation because …'

Followed by the chorus: '*I've never liked him.*'

I couldn't possibly blame them. I don't like him either, for all the reasons outlined above.

So why am I meeting him, in secret, every chance I get?

My dictionary defines addiction as: 'the condition of being enslaved to a habit or practice to such an extent that its cessation causes severe trauma'. It's as good an explanation as any. I'm not sure I experienced severe trauma when we split, but there were a lot of wet pillows on my bed for months afterwards. And even when the pillows were dry again, the bed felt so empty, so bleak. I couldn't envisage a replacement for him there, even if I did go to the pictures or eat out with the occasional nice guy. The occasional nice guy never made it up the stairs. He just seemed to have the wrong pheromones. He wasn't Luke.

He didn't size me up and strip me with his eyes within a second of looking at me. He didn't do that slow burn over the table linen that had me gagging for it by the time the dessert menu arrived. There wasn't that constant low-level possibility of being thrown up against a wall, whenever and wherever, and taken.

Those things were part and parcel of Luke. If only they didn't come with the cruelty and the self-absorption and the rest of it.

It helped that we didn't live in the same town, and I thought I was over it until he walked into my estate agency, looking for details of executive one-bed apartments by the harbour.

I was in the back office at the time, so I didn't see him come in. I walked out with a sheaf of mailing lists to put into envelopes and almost dropped them all over the floor. I thought perhaps I'd been shot. That face, that hair, that tall athletic body. The shock of the initial bullet through my heart spread to infect my crotch with unwanted waves of sense-memory. The things he'd done to me ... wicked, delicious things that nobody had done since. I couldn't look at his fingers without recalling their explorations, nor hear his soft-spoken voice without the words mutating into the hot-breathed obscenities he used to whisper into my ear.

He looked up and I gripped the mailshots harder, determined to look unflustered and indifferent.

'Ruthie.' That smile. Why was it having the same effect on me it used to have? I looked for hatred and bitterness, found only lust. 'I was just asking after you. I hoped you'd still be here. Do you mind?'

He dismissed my colleague, who vacated his chair for me and disappeared, taking over my envelope-stuffing task.

'Of all the estate agents in all the world ...' I said, trying to keep control of my wobbly voice, keep it calm. 'What are you doing here?'

'I got a promotion to the local office.'

'You aren't moving here?'

'On the contrary. So I need your finest selection of bachelor pads. You're looking well.'

The change of tack steered me off course. I think, to my horror, I might have blushed.

'Bachelor pads,' I said, studiedly ignoring the compliment, clicking my mouse ostentatiously and scrolling through pages of listings.

'I'm just grateful you didn't knock my block off,' he said, as if to himself. 'Can't really ask for more than that.'

'What's your upper price limit?'

'It's wonderful to see you again. I think about you a lot. About how we were ... I was so stupid. There's never been anyone like you.'

'Price limit?'

'Oh, I don't really have one. I'm loaded. Just give me anything you've got that's fucking huge with a sea view.'

'You're still an insufferable show-off then.'

'Yeah, you know me. What have you got?'

He leaned forwards, trying to get a view of my computer screen. I caught the whiff of his aftershave, the same one he used to wear. I had to pinch my lips together so as not to groan at the procession of images of us fucking that ran through my head. I clamped my thighs. My knickers were wet. Damn him to hell.

'New development – Anchor Quay. Seems to be popular with the more-money-than-sense crowd. There's a penthouse you might like.'

'Take me there.'

I stared at him. 'What?'

'I want to look at it. I won't have time unless I do it

now. I've got meetings all afternoon. Set up an appointment.'

'I don't have to. It's vacant. I've got the keys.' This is what came out of my mouth, instead of my intended *Fuck off*.

'Even better. So what are we waiting for?'

Me to get a grip, presumably. But the grip remained ungotten. I found the keys, grabbed my handbag and gave a brief explanation to the office manager, then we were on the street, striding up towards the harbour under a sun whose very heat seemed to be warning me off.

I couldn't help scoping the crowds of daytime shoppers for people I knew who might see us together and gasp and gossip. Luke's behaviour had been the talk of my little section of the town for weeks. He was pretty much on a par with the Antichrist around here.

'You've got some front,' I muttered, once we were off the main drag and heading across the cobbles towards the quayside. 'Rolling up and expecting me to talk to you after the way you … ugh.'

He put his hand on my shoulder. *He put his hand on my shoulder!* How dared he? But I didn't shrug it off. I half-expected the fabric of my jacket to burn through where he touched it. I think I was trembling.

'Ruthie,' he said, in that gentle, hypnotic, evil way of his. 'Ruthie, Ruthie, Ruthie. I know I can't make that up to you. I know I broke your heart, and I can't tell you how sorry I am.'

'No you didn't! Don't flatter yourself. My heart's perfectly fine, thanks.'

'Good. That's great. So you're seeing someone?'

Busted! But I could always lie.

'Yeah, yeah, I am actually. It's fantastic. I'm really happy.'

'Well, I'm really happy for you. You deserve a good man.'

The hand came off my shoulder. Had my fake boyfriend done his work? We arrived at the apartment complex and I showed him through the airy plant-filled atrium to the lifts.

Being alone in a lift with Luke was a test of resolve. He stood close to me, the sleeves of our respective linen jackets touching, his heat pouring over me, his smell filling me up. We'd snogged in a lift before. We'd come pretty close to shagging, if I remembered correctly. I didn't want to remember correctly. I didn't want to remember at all.

I was light-headed when the lift doors pinged open at the top floor.

'Here it is,' I said with exaggerated bonhomie, fitting the key to the lock. 'The penthouse apartment.'

I let him in before me, giving him a good few moments to get out of my personal space.

'I like it,' he said. He would. All that smoked glass, clean lines, blah, blah. It was impersonal enough for his tastes.

Within a minute, he had slid open the balcony doors and stood looking over the ledge at the harbour and the vast blue sea beyond. 'It's wonderful. Come and look.'

'I've seen it.'

'I know you have, but come and see it again.'

I had this presentiment that he wasn't just talking about the view. My good sense held back, but my treacherous feet ignored it, dragging me over to him.

Beside him, leaning against the railings, high above the street, I seemed to have also risen above my inhibitions. Nobody could see us up here. Nobody could hear us. We were alone. Together.

'You're still angry with me, aren't you?' he said after a pause to take in the clean air and the idyllic view.

'Wouldn't you be?'

'Yeah. I would. I behaved like a dick. But I don't want you to be angry with me.'

'I feel so terribly sorry for you. Must be awful when people dislike you for behaving like a dick. What a cross to bear.'

'I didn't give you the chance to take your anger out on me either. I just disappeared. Maybe I should give you that chance now.'

'What do you mean?'

43

'Hit me.'

'What?'

'Go on. Slap my face. Really hard. Give me what you've been fantasising about since I hurt you.'

It wasn't a good idea but I didn't care. The temptation was too strong. I stepped away from the balcony railing at the same time as he did, swung back my arm and dealt him the hardest, loudest, most brilliantly satisfying smack to the side of his face anyone could describe or imagine.

After I did it, I laughed with delight and jumped up and down.

And he smiled.

And took hold of my wrist.

And made me put the flat of my palm against the hot red patch.

And I stopped breathing.

'Don't,' I said, but it was really just the touch of my tongue on the roof of my mouth, not a real word.

'You want me to. You've been wanting to touch me since I walked into your office. Let it happen.'

'I don't …'

'Fight me then. But you'll only be fighting yourself.'

I made a weak attempt to pull back, but he held fast, knowing his power.

What would one shag matter? One last chance to drown in sex before Mr Nice Guy triumphed and I bought myself a vibrating love bullet? I held all the cards now. I was over him. I could come and then go.

'Fuck you,' I said. 'OK, then, you can have my body. But that's all you're getting. No more than that.'

'It's enough for starters,' he said.

The kissing was everything I remembered and more, a slow, spinning trip into the heart of my desire. With his urgent tongue and demanding lips, he awakened my nipples, my clit, my cunt, without having to touch any of them.

But when he did …

On my back, on the show-home bed, I gathered all that sensation greedily into me, wanting to feel everything I had missed for so long. The way he held me, close, one hand on my arse, lips roving over neck and shoulders. Then there was the way he teased my nipples, tongue tip and thumb pad working in devilish unison, making me arch my back and try to trap him in my thighs. There was also his unerring speed in locating my clit, a touch that was feathery or firm as required, fingers whose length and sensitivity fitted my cunt like a glove, drawing forth more juice than I thought I had in me.

'You're still the horniest bastard in town.' He had laid me waste, my jacket and skirt flung aside, shirt undone, bra cups down, knickers around my knees.

'That's one thing that'll never change,' he said, his hand plunging between my thighs while the other groped over the side of the bed for his jacket.

It was so good to see him on top of me, his head ducked close to mine, his lean body pinning me to the bed. It was a place I had often wished I could go back to, despite myself. I slid my hands into his red-gold hair and put up my lips for another kiss.

He wrestled blindly with his jacket for another minute or so then reared up in triumph, the condom retrieved. Had he planned this?

'You planned this.'

'Of course.'

'You came to my office thinking you could get me into bed.'

'And so I did.'

'You …'

'Oh, stop it. You want me to fuck you. Just lie back and spread your legs, Ruthie, and I'll give you what you want.'

'What I want is for you to go away.'

'No it isn't.' His fingers curled inside my labia, rubbing against my clit. 'This doesn't want me to go away. And neither does this.' One finger speared my cunt, quickly joined by another. 'Does it?'

I shut my eyes and rode on the feeling. I had to take the edge off. I had to have him. 'My body can have what it wants. Just this once.'

The intensity built, pre-quakes rumbling in the inner distance as his fingers did their dirty work.

'Of course, just this once. If that's what you want.'

Oh, it was good to have him on me again, to feel that skin and share that heartbeat. My body stretched out and purred. My will conceded the fight.

He seized that critical moment and replaced fingers with cock.

The size of him again, the stretching width and unforgiving length, reminding my cunt with instant efficacy of everything it had missed – oh, it was cruel. It had taken me so long to forget the first time he left me and now I had fresh memories to replace those I had worked to erase.

'Remember this?' he said, pausing to drive the impression home, to burn it on my mind. 'Oh, you remember it. How we used to go at it, Ruthie. Hammer and tongs, anywhere, everywhere. How you used to sob for mercy under me. Does he do that for you?'

'Who?'

'As I thought.' He smiled patronisingly and began the job of bending me to him, enslaving me anew with each thrust.

I lay beneath him on the pristine bed, then I was on top, then I was on all fours, then I was ... well, I can't remember the endless permutations and I lost count of the number of orgasms. I recall a kind of sweaty blur, the strained skin on his forehead and the manic look in his eyes as he pumped away, my body melting slowly into his.

Only the intrusive pip, pip of my mobile phone interrupted our morning of rekindled lust. I was late for a viewing in Alderley Crescent.

'Shit! Have we really been shagging for an hour and a half?' I retrieved my bra from the light fitting and wrestled it on.

'That was a warm-up compared to what we used to get up to,' said Luke. He stilled my frantic fumbling, took my hands and pulled me close. 'You can't tell me that was the last time. Your body will hate you for it, and so will mine.'

'Stupid bloody body,' I mumbled, but I knew this would happen again, and not just once, but many, many times.

He bought the flat.

In the months since he moved in, we've fucked in every room and on the balcony. He calls me, I go there, he uses my pussy (or whichever orifice he has in mind), I use his cock, I leave. I get orgasms and pulled muscles and afterglow.

That's good, isn't it? That makes the uneasy sense of being at the beck and call of a narcissistic bastard worthwhile, doesn't it?

If it was good, though, I'd be able to tell people about it, and I can't ever tell anyone about it.

'This has to stop.' Perhaps I shouldn't say this mid-kiss with my knickers around my knees. It takes some of the force from the statement. But he looks so good with his shirt undone to his navel and those tight-fitting jeans and bare feet … how was I supposed to resist?

'What has to stop?' His hand delves between my denuded pussy lips. 'You're fucking soaked, Ruthie. What do you want to stop?' He rubs my clit, as if to tell me I'm being ridiculous.

'This. Us. I can't do it any more.'

'You can't do it? What, you can't fuck? Oh yes you can. And I'll prove it to you.' His fingertips circle and swish, bringing me closer to incoherence and surrender.

'Oh don't, don't …'

He takes them away and I almost grab his wrist to force their replacement. Talk about mixed signals, but there's no sense in this, no reasoning with my pussy. He holds my arms by my sides and sighs, bending his head to mine.

'You say this every time,' he reminds me.

'This time I mean it. I've turned down so many opportunities to go out and socialise so I can meet you instead. I've put my life on hold for you. I need to get past you and move on.'

'You need closure?' He says the word mockingly, his tone installing the air quotes while his fingers are otherwise occupied.

'Yeah.'

'You want your cunt to close up? You won't find

another man who can fuck you like this, Ruthie. You need my cock, and you know it.'

Something about his self-satisfied certainty kick starts my resolve. 'No I don't. I don't need your cock. My fingers can do the job just as well, and if I want a little extra, there's plenty of online toyshops that can help out. See, there's one problem with your cock – it's attached to you.'

He's silent for a moment, looking as if he's been slapped. 'Is this about commitment?' he asks eventually. 'You want someone to take you to the cinema between shags? I can do that.'

'You have the most revolting attitude …'

If only he had the most revolting face and body to go with it. But he's doing that 'melt you with my hurt blue eyes' thing that drives me mad.

'I know, Ruthie, I know. I need help to be a better person. Help me.'

This is a blatant ploy to get me back on track for the hard ride he has been looking forward to. I know this; he knows this.

I go along with it anyway. But this will be the last time. It really will. 'Shut up, you liar. You just want to get my legs back open.'

He flutters fingertips over my inner thighs, whispering them apart. 'You want it.' He drips his poison into my willing ear. 'You want it too.'

'Just this time, then no more.'

'Of course. But if it's going to be the last time, I want the full works.' He finds me wet between the legs again.

'The full works?'

'Yeah.' He is lazy with my clit, stroking slowly while his hot breath fans my ear. 'I'm having your arse tonight.'

Words that always strike a sick and fearful thrill.

He pats it for emphasis, lightly at first then, when I squirm, he smacks harder. 'What do you think of that?'

He has hands fore and aft now, fingers burrowing between lips and cleft. I shift on the balls of my feet, lifting myself to give him better access while he holds me upright with a shoulder to lean on.

'What you want,' I breathe. 'Whatever you want – it's the last time.'

I drape my arms around his neck and give in to the urgent fingering, knowing it won't end until my cunt is contracting around his bunched digits and I am weak from climax.

'One last suck on it,' he croons, putting a hand on my shoulder to push me to my knees.

I bury that cock in my mouth, tasting its last traces, the ridges and curvature I have come to know so well. I enfold it in the heat of my mouth, wrap my tongue around it, give it the final bath.

He pulls out before I can drink my final draught though, and then I am head down, arse up on the bed, elbows and knees bent, waiting for the cold sweet kiss of the lube.

'You think you can just walk away,' he says, joining me on the bed, running hands all over my presented cheeks. 'But you know I won't make it easy for you. What are you going to do when you wake up in the middle of the night, needing my cock?'

'I never do that.'

'You're a liar.'

I am a liar. He smacks my bottom again, really hard this time. I want to look around and see if there's a handprint, but I wouldn't be able to see.

His lubricated finger parts my cheeks and twirls into my back passage, that place only he has been. I move back, pushing on to him, a ritualistic response my body has learned over these months.

When he inserts his cock, after much exploring and clit-rubbing, I brace myself for the familiar moment of burn before the slow expansion of pleasure.

'You belong here, Ruthie,' he says, easing me through it, continuing forwards until his balls rest against the underside of my bottom. 'This is what you're made for.'

'It's not enough.' I am full, held in absolute thrall, submitting completely to his control.

'This? Not enough?' He pulls out and jolts it back up to the hilt, once, twice, three times. 'Not enough for you?'

'Sex. Is not enough.'

He pulls my hair, holds me by a tight ponytail until my scalp fizzes. 'It's enough for you.'

I give up. I give him my arse, unimpeded, freely. He takes it, takes as much of it as he can, greedy and ferocious in his sodomising. I come with fingers on my clit, mine the first time, the second time his, then he finishes inside me, an orgasmic swansong that lays me flat on the covers.

After he pulls out, he holds my cheeks apart and examines his work while I lie spinning in subspace, waiting for thought to return.

'Do you remember the first time we did this?'

'Of course. I had to take that conference call with your cock in my arse.'

'That was amazing. I was shoving it all the way in with you on all fours talking into your phone about which survey you recommended.'

'When I came I had to pretend I had a caller on the other line.'

'What about that time over the balcony? When that yacht flashed a semaphore message at us?'

'I wish I knew semaphore. I still wonder what it said.'

'Can you really give me up?'

'Yes. I can give you up. It's the sex I'll miss.'

***

I'm at a party with my friends. It's the first time in ages I haven't sloped off early to have sex with Luke.

I'm thinking of him as that restless time arrives. Could I?

I head for the toilets, deciding on a bit of self-pleasure to medicate away the obsession. I put out my hand to turn the knob but my fingers slip off and the door opens of its own accord, revealing ...

'Luke.'

Those eyes floor me, roving up and down, ravenous. 'Ruthie.'

We both look down the stairs and across the landing, checking for watchful guests. There are none.

He pulls me into the bathroom and locks the door.

Instantly we are joined, arms locked around each other, legs twisting and twining, mouths jammed tight.

He yanks down his trousers and pants and sits on the closed lid of the toilet, pulling me down on to his lap. My skirt is rucked up, knickers shoved aside, his hands are everywhere, inside my top, in my hair, on my arse.

I sit on his cock and feel it glide in, fitting so perfectly, clicking into place like a missing part of me. He holds me by my bottom and guides me into a slow grind, catching my lower lip with his teeth, nipping at it. My clit rubs against his pelvis. I begin my ascent.

'This is the last time,' I hiss as he squeezes my cheeks hard.

'Of course,' he says.

In the Middle of Nowhere
Gwen Masters

I took another sip of my beer and watched the stars. I was lying on the porch at our summer cabin in the middle of nowhere, out where earthly lights didn't compete with the heavenly ones. I was sure the stars were always up there, but I had never seen so many. I watched as one of them lost its anchor and fell in a gentle arc, crossing the horizon before blinking out.

'Cheers,' I said aloud, and lifted my beer in salute.

This was exactly where I needed to be. Relaxation was long overdue and, besides that, I needed some serious time to think since my life had turned itself upside down and inside out.

* * *

Keith and I had been together just long enough to read each other's moods. We understood one another in the ways that only a couple who has been completely open and honest can. That's why he didn't hesitate to tell me about his fantasies.

'I have always wanted to see my woman with another man,' Keith announced one night as he lay in bed beside me. He was still trying to catch his breath.

The thought of two men was always a fantasy of mine, too. My body instantly responded again, even though I had just been satisfied over and over. 'Why?' I asked.

'I want to see a woman of mine take all the pleasure she can possibly stand,' he said. 'I guess it helps that I don't have a jealous streak. As long as you're doing it in front of me, it's not cheating, and I don't mind whatever you might want to do. I like being able to let you fulfil all your fantasies, and not have to worry about you going elsewhere to do that.'

That was not what I expected to hear. I sat up and looked at him in the near-darkness. I knew Keith was always very laid-back when we were around his friends or mine, even the male friends who liked to flirt from time to time. But I always chalked that up to him simply trusting me, not to his very nature.

'You don't get jealous?' I asked. 'At all?'

'Never have, no.'

'Even if your woman was with someone else, it wouldn't bother you?'

'It would bother me if you did it with someone else and I wasn't included. I think that would be cheating. But if you can do it right in front of me, that's not cheating, right?'

'I guess so.'

'So I would like to see you do it.'

'But what if I like him more than I like you?'

Keith shrugged in the darkness. 'That's the chance I have to take.'

'So you mean you would be willing to take a chance that I might leave you?'

'If you're going to leave, you're going to leave. There's nothing I can do to stop you.'

'But you don't have to bring it on by allowing me to be with other men, right?'

Keith sighed. 'You don't understand that kind of life-style,' he said quietly.

'What? An open relationship?'

'No. It's not exactly open. It's more like swinging. Doing it together.'

'What if you choose to have another woman involved?'

'Would that bother you?'

'You're damn right it would!' I was on the verge of furious at the thought. Keith looked at me in the darkness. I could make out the outline of his jaw but I couldn't see his eyes. I flicked on the bedside lamp and he immediately threw an arm across his face.

'Shit!'

'Do you want another woman?'

'No! I never said anything about that. You were the one who brought it up.'

'So you would be OK with me being with another man.'

'Yes,' he said with strained patience.

'But you wouldn't be jealous.'

'No.'

'Why not?'

Keith threw his hand down and glared at me. 'Because I'm not the jealous type. I already told you that. What is this, selective hearing?'

I glared right back at him.

'Well?' he asked.

'Well, what?'

'Do you want to do something like that?'

I flopped back down on the bed. Now Keith was the one who sat up to study me. 'I don't know,' I said softly. 'It's a good fantasy. But what I need in real life is much more important.'

'What do you need?'

'I need a man who will give a damn if I'm with someone else. I want a man who will barely restrain himself from kicking the ass of the guy at the bar who dares to hit on me while I'm with him. I want a man who will deliver that ass-kicking if the guy dares to hit on me twice. I want a man who will proudly tell everybody I'm his girl and that is that, period, end of story. I want to feel protected.'

'You want a man to be jealous?'

'Not jealous,' I said, thinking hard. 'Possessive, maybe.'

'So now you're an object. A possession. Great.'

I rolled away from him and faced the wall. 'You don't understand.'

'Honey,' Keith said, touching my shoulder. 'It's not that I'm not proud of you. I'm happy to call you mine. I think we make a great team. I love you with all my heart. I just don't see the jealousy bit. I've never been the jealous type. If you want to be with another man, fine. Do it right in front of me, so we can both enjoy it. Just don't do it behind my back. That's all I ask.'

'I would never,' I said vehemently, and Keith cut me off.

'I know. I trust you.'

'I don't think I can do it in front of you, either.'

'We can try,' he suggested.

'How?'

'I have a friend,' he said. 'His name is Jake.'

***

The moment I laid eyes on Jake, I knew I was in big trouble.

Jake was tall and lean, with an athlete's body and beautiful green eyes. His hair was far too long, almost shaggy, but looked soft as a baby's locks. He had a great tan and a smile that showed perfect teeth. His laugh was infectious and he moved with a grace that belied his rough-and-tumble attitude.

Perhaps if Keith had never mentioned Jake's name, I never would have looked at him as a potential lover. But he had, and for many nights the idea of this man had been in my head. Now that I was seeing him in the flesh, my body was already responding in certain ways that were inappropriate – or appropriate, depending on how I looked at the situation.

Keith and Jake embraced there in the parking lot of the coliseum. Inside, the crowd was rowdy and loud – the show had just started. We had tickets, but it had taken us a bit too long to find each other in the many parking lots around the venue. Out among the many cars, the scene was quiet. The two men clapped each other on the back and talked about the usual things – how's that truck holding up, how is your momma doing, would you like to meet my girlfriend?

Jake turned to me. He gave me a quick once-over, but that was enough. His eyes met mine and the appreciation in them was evident. I blushed as he looked at me.

'The pleasure is all mine,' he said, and I blushed harder.

Keith looked at me, then at Jake. He sized up the situation and cast a knowing grin in my direction.

'Let's ditch the show and go out to dinner,' he said.

* * *

Dinner was at a bistro just outside of town, where the locals rarely bothered to venture and the out-of-towners seemed to have missed in favour of the concert going on down the street. We were practically alone in the restaurant. I twirled my fork through the spaghetti and listened as the two men talked about football and travel and music and everything in between. I occasionally spoke, but mostly I was just quiet, taking it all in while the two of them caught up on what life had brought them in the six months since they had last seen each other.

'I've missed you,' Keith said once, and Jake smiled at him. The look that passed between them was that of two old friends who are closer than brothers, who have spent their lives looking after one another. Watching them together made me feel warm from the inside out.

'I missed you too,' Jake said.

Keith excused himself from the table shortly after that, and Jake turned to me. 'You've been quiet all night,' he said.

'I've been listening.'

'Do you always do that?'

'Do what?'

'Listen so intently? You don't miss much. You seem comfortable as an observer. Either that, or you have something serious weighing on your mind.'

I looked at him in surprise. 'You read people very well.'

Jake smiled at me and took a sip of wine. 'Sometimes.'

'There's nothing on my mind,' I said. We both knew I was lying. Jake didn't say a word – he simply sat back in his chair and swirled the wine in his glass, staring straight at me.

I tried not to squirm under his gaze. It was impossible. 'I've got a few things on my mind,' I admitted.

'I know how Keith is,' he said, and I looked at him in surprise. Jake went on. 'I know why he wanted us to meet. I know what's on his mind, so I'm pretty sure what's on yours.'

I took a big drink of my own wine. 'So he's done this before?'

Jake shrugged. 'I don't think so, no. But I know he's always wanted to.'

'Why me?' I asked.

'Because you were open enough to consider it.'

'But I'm not.'

'You're not?'

'I can't get past the lack of jealousy.'

Jake shifted in his chair. His eyes dropped to his wine

62

glass. 'Some people just aren't jealous. I know it's hard to believe, but Keith really is one of those people. It must be hard to adjust.'

'Did other women find it hard to adjust?'

Jake smiled and answered carefully, 'I think they just weren't right for Keith.'

'That's a diplomatic answer.'

'I'm a diplomatic kind of guy.'

'Are you a jealous kind of guy?' The question came out of nowhere. I hadn't even known I would ask it until the question was already out in the open. Jake raised an eyebrow. He blushed and, for once, looked as though he didn't have an answer. He looked over my shoulder.

'Hey, look who's back,' he said, and refused to meet my eyes for the rest of the meal.

***

That night in bed, Keith asked me what I thought of Jake.

'He's a very nice man,' I said honestly. 'I like his manner. And he's very talkative but he doesn't monopolise the conversation until you start talking about sports.'

Keith laughed. 'He's the sports fanatic, definitely.'

'I like him,' I said.

'How much do you like him?'

It was very odd to hear that question from Keith,

knowing there was no jealousy behind it. There wasn't even a hint of it in his tone. He was simply curious as to how I felt, and of course, there might be an agenda behind that curiosity.

'A lot,' I said frankly.

Keith cuddled me closer to his side. 'Really?'

'Yeah.'

'Enough to like him as more than a friend?'

I bit my lip. This was the strangest conversation I had ever had with anyone. 'If I were not with you, maybe. But I'm a one-man kind of woman. You know that. I'm not going to look elsewhere. Even if you encourage me to do so.'

Keith sat up in bed. I thought he was reaching for something on the nightstand, but he was actually reaching for his robe. He shrugged it on and walked out of the room. The door slammed behind him.

I lay there for a moment, completely stunned. I didn't know how to react. I couldn't see the situation the same way he did. I couldn't imagine doing what he wanted me to do, even though the fantasy was huge in the back of my mind. Sometimes I fantasised about more than two men – sometimes my fantasies involved gang-bangs, strings of men who wanted only one thing and took it, over and over and over. But could I actually do those things? The fantasies stopped at the point where the reality began. The fantasy was great but the reality might not be.

But maybe that wasn't what was really bothering me. Maybe it was the fact that Keith wanted the fantasy so badly, he wasn't willing to see my point of view. I simply wasn't comfortable with being with anyone else. Why couldn't he accept that?

Everything else about him was perfect. Why was I so intent on having a jealous man?

I lay there for a very long time before Keith came back to the bedroom.

'I'm sorry,' he said as he crawled in beside me.

I didn't answer. Soon his breathing was deep and even, but I was awake for hours before I could finally join him in sleep.

***

Keith awoke the next morning in a very pensive mood. We hung around the house and said little to each other during those hours when he was thinking things through. Finally, he came to me and wrapped his arms around my shoulders.

'If you aren't comfortable with it,' he said, 'I won't bring it up again.'

I was startled by his change in attitude. I had a surprise for him, too. 'I thought about it last night,' I admitted. 'And I decided that I would try it.'

Keith and I looked at each other, neither of us knowing

how to respond. Finally, Keith cleared his throat and kissed my forehead. 'Seems we love each other enough to compromise,' he said.

I took him down to the kitchen floor right then and there and had my way with him. Our lunch burned on the stove. I was making love to Keith, but Jake was in the back of my mind.

* * *

The next night Jake came over for dinner.

I had a whole spread for us – chicken with mushroom sauce, asparagus steamed to perfection, mashed potatoes and carrots that were golden with brown sugar. Fresh bread cooled on the sideboard. A good bottle of wine was chilling in the cooler.

Jake walked up behind me in the kitchen and kissed me on the cheek. 'It's good to see you,' he said.

We sat down to dinner and I watched the men talk. Keith kept looking at me, more animated than he had been in a long time. Jake was drinking the wine like it was going out of style. Keith watched him with growing concern.

'Are you all right?' he asked once, and Jake glanced at me before he answered.

'Of course I'm fine.'

I was puzzled at Jake's attitude. He had said he knew

how Keith was, and he had agreed to have dinner at our home – surely he knew the kind of things Keith and I had discussed since the first time we had dinner? He kept looking at me as though he wanted to say something, but he couldn't find the proper words or the proper time.

As I was cleaning the kitchen, Keith went out onto the porch. Jake leaned on the counter and looked at me. 'You're not OK with this,' he said bluntly.

I didn't play dumb. 'I told him I was OK with it.'

'That doesn't mean you are.'

I turned to Jake. His green eyes were bright with too much alcohol. He looked at me with a very guarded expression, but his body told a story he couldn't hide. He was tense from head to toe. He drained the wine. I watched as he set the glass on the counter. He picked up the bottle and tipped it in my direction.

'I think I'll just drink from the well,' he said, and turned it up. I watched his throat move as he drank the wine. He sighed and looked at me, then motioned with the bottle. 'Want some?'

I stepped forwards. Now that I was so close to him I could smell his cologne, something deep and woodsy and masculine. Jake moved the bottle away from between us, giving me even more opportunity to come closer. His free hand came around to the small of my back. The first touch was electric, almost frightening, and I suddenly knew that I wasn't ready for this after all.

Keith walked into the room. Jake put more pressure on my back and pulled me closer. I looked at Keith as he sank down into one of the kitchen chairs. I watched his eyes for any trace of jealousy, any sign that he was uncomfortable, but there was none. He looked at us with something that could only be approval.

I stared at him. Minutes ticked by on the clock. Keith watched us closely. His eyes took in everything, from our toes to our hair and then back down. Jake tipped up the bottle again, and that was the only time Keith looked concerned about what was happening right in front of him in his kitchen.

'You're drinking fast,' Keith commented.

Jake looked at me. 'I'm not drinking fast enough,' he said. The expression in his eyes was unreadable. He pulled me tight against him, hard enough that I could feel what the wine and the tension had done to him. His cock was hard as a rock. His whole body was tense. Jake didn't take his eyes away from mine.

I was very aware of Keith. He sat there and watched his friend pull me tight against him. He knew what was coming, and he wasn't about to protest. I knew he wouldn't. My body leaped at the thought of having Jake. My heart fell at the fact that I actually could.

I twined my fingers through Jake's hair and pulled him down for a kiss.

Jake moaned as soon as my lips touched his. His

tongue found mine. He tasted like wine. I kissed him slowly. I took my time and explored every inch of his mouth. Jake's arm came around me as he kissed me back. I was wrapped up in his arms, wrapped up in his scent, wrapped up in what he was making me feel – a deep and low trembling, right between my thighs.

Jake uttered a curse against my lips. He pushed me back against the counter. He kissed me harder, all doubts forgotten. The fire that raged in me was obviously in him, too – he kissed me with what was almost desperation. I twined both hands into his hair as he settled himself firmly against me. My breath was harsh. His heart was beating even harder than mine was.

It was only when I opened my eyes and pulled away to catch my breath that I remembered Keith was in the room. He sat on the chair at the other end of the kitchen. His eyes were bright with something I recognised. Keith was horny as hell.

My face flooded with heat. Jake kissed his way down the side of my neck and then back up. He found my ear and the gentle stroke of his tongue made me shiver. I stared at Keith while Jake worked magic that made my nipples hard and my body wet. Keith stared right back.

Jake thrust up against me, one time only, and whispered into my ear, 'I would never let another man do this to you.'

My heart and my body were plunged into confusion.

Anger swamped me. Part of me wanted to pull Jake closer and another part of me wanted to push him away. Guilt was a violent tempest within my head. I closed my eyes so I didn't have to see Keith.

But I couldn't shake the fact that I wanted Jake.

Jake was the one who stopped. He ran his fingers through my hair, kissed me hard and then slowly took a step back. He looked right at me while he spoke to Keith. 'I can't do this.'

Keith looked from Jake to me. He didn't seem surprised at all. Jake was breathing hard. He closed his eyes and rested his forehead against mine for a long moment.

'I'm the jealous kind,' Jake said.

Keith did look surprised then. The edge of anger surfaced in his eyes. Though he buried it quickly, the quick blush on his face said he knew I'd seen it.

Jake stepped away from me and handed me the wine. The bottle was cool but where his hand had been was almost slippery with warmth. He shook his head once, slowly, then turned and walked out of the kitchen. He went out the front door.

'He's too drunk to drive,' I told Keith.

He didn't meet my eyes. 'He will be fine.'

I ran to the front door. Jake was pulling out of the driveway. He gunned the engine and tore down the road without looking back. There was no way I could have stopped him.

70

I turned to see Keith standing there behind me.

'Is that what you wanted to see?' I almost hissed.

'Yes.'

I threw myself at him like a wildcat. Keith caught my arms and we both tumbled to the floor, right there in the open doorway. The wine bottle thumped on the floor and then rolled across the hardwood, spilling drops of wine as it went. Keith yanked my shirt open. I pulled his jeans down. Within seconds, he was buried inside me, thrusting hard into the wetness Jake had created.

It was the best fuck of my life.

***

I could not get Jake off my mind. Keith called a few times but Jake never answered his phone, and didn't return the messages. Days went by and Keith and I settled back into our routine. We rarely mentioned Jake and we never mentioned what had happened that night. It sat between us like the elephant in the room that nobody mentions, but that nobody can ignore.

It was a few days later when Keith came into the bedroom and saw me packing the smallest of my suitcases. 'Where are you going?' he asked.

I was quiet as I pushed in a pair of sandals. 'I'm taking a few days up at the cabin,' I said. 'I need time to think.'

Keith glared at me. He went from calm and collected

to furious in the time it took me to answer him. 'Like hell you are,' he said. 'Like hell you do.'

I wasn't expecting that. Keith had taken my silence in his stride these last few days. Surely he knew what was going through my head? Did he really think everything would continue as it had been?

'I feel as though I have done something horrible,' I said to him, and I was chagrined at the tears that pricked my eyes. I had sworn that I wouldn't cry over this. I took a deep breath. 'I feel as though I have betrayed you, and myself, and even Jake. I need time to sort things out in my head and I can't do that here with you.'

Keith grabbed my wrist as I reached to close the suit-case. He shoved it off the bed. Clothes went everywhere. I didn't move as he stood over me.

'You said you were OK with what you did,' Keith said. 'You were OK with it. What if Jake hadn't stopped? You would have fucked him just like you fucked me as soon as he left.'

My face flooded with heat. 'I thought that was what you wanted,' I said to him.

'I didn't want to lose you over him!' Keith hollered.

'That's what I warned you might happen!' I hollered right back. 'I told you I wasn't comfortable with it! I told you I was a one-man woman! I told you those things and you kept insisting. You were so certain I would like it that you pushed and pushed and pushed and now this is how I feel and I can't help it. I don't know what to think or what to do or what to want any more!'

Keith stared at me with wide eyes. For the first time, I saw fear in them.

'Your lack of jealousy is not something I can handle,' I said softly. 'You show your love in so many ways. But if you really loved me, wouldn't you want me to be with you, and nobody else?'

'If I really loved you,' Keith countered, 'it seems to me I would want you to have as much pleasure as possible.'

I took a deep breath. 'In this whole situation,' I said, 'the one thing you haven't taken into account is that maybe being with you and nobody else – being your girlfriend, and not being touched by any man but you – is the most pleasurable thing I can imagine.'

Keith sank down on the bed. He let go of my wrist. My hand throbbed, and I rubbed it while Keith watched me.

'I'm sorry I hurt you,' he said.

'It's all right. I know you didn't mean it.'

'I don't mean just your wrist. I'm sorry for all of this.'

Keith and I looked at each other. Finally, he looked down at the suitcase, but not before I caught the tears in his eyes.

'I think we both need time to think,' I said.

Keith nodded. 'You're right.'

I should have been happy that he agreed with me, but instead I felt as though I had lost something very special in return for winning the argument. I sat down on his lap and wrapped my arms around his shoulders. Keith buried his face against my neck. We sat there like that until the sun started to fall from the sky.

* * *

I watched the stars and thought about the last few weeks. I knew I couldn't handle making that fantasy a reality. If kissing Jake in the kitchen had caused so much turmoil, there was no way that I could handle doing anything more. But pleasing a man was so important to me, and I wanted to give Keith the fantasies he longed to fulfil. He had trusted me enough to share them, and this was how I rewarded him?

It seemed we were at an impasse, with no compromise possible.

I lay there on the deck and watched the stars twinkle. I listened to the crickets and night birds. I watched a plane glide across the sky, its lights flashing red in the midst of black and white. I studied the Milky Way. I tried to count stars, a fruitless exercise in frustration, but it kept me from thinking about other things.

I heard the sound of tyres on gravel while the vehicle was still miles away. I listened to it with less than a quarter of my attention, sure it would pull into a driveway long before it reached me. I was surprised when I heard the whine of the tyres come up the hill to the cabin. I sat up and watched the headlights make their way through the trees. A startled raccoon fled through the light, ran through the underbrush and scampered up a tree, where it disappeared into the leaves.

The truck pulled into the drive. I took another sip of my beer. I was surprised when the lights flickered off. I was even more surprised when a man stepped out of the truck and walked towards me. It was only when he stepped through a shaft of moonlight that I realised who he was.

I should have known.

'Keith told me you might be out here,' Jake said.

I held out the beer. He took it and drank the rest in one long swallow. We sat side by side on the porch and looked out at the silhouettes of the trees.

'How is he?' I asked.

Jake picked at a spot on his jeans. 'He's all right. He knows everybody handled the situation badly.'

'I don't blame him. I don't blame anybody.'

Jake chuckled ruefully. 'That's the problem with things like this. There is nobody to blame. It's easier if there is someone who can be held accountable.'

I got up to get another beer. I pulled two longnecks out of the cooler and handed one to Jake. We twisted off the tops and sat in companionable silence, watching the night close in around us.

'Why are you here?' I asked.

'I don't know.'

I nodded, grateful for his honesty. 'Keith knows you're here?'

'Yeah. He invited me to come out here. He said you might want some company.'

I looked at Jake. He looked at me.

'I didn't ask,' he said softly. 'I just took it for what it was.'

I looked away, unsure of what to say. Anger and sadness warred for top billing. What the hell was happening here? I needed time to think, not time to spend with anyone else.

'I'm still his girlfriend,' I said. 'Does he know that?'

'Are you?' Jake asked bluntly.

I looked up at the stars. 'I don't know. I don't know who belongs where any more.'

'I think he's already made up his mind,' Jake said, so softly I could barely hear him. I pretended not to hear him at all, even as my heart beat a tattoo of fear in my chest. After a time the fear was replaced with a quick flash of anger, then with the same sadness I had felt for days and days.

'How long are you here?' I asked.

Jake took a long drink of his beer. 'That depends on you.'

I stood up on the porch and offered my hand. He held it a little too long after he stood up. We looked at each other and the electricity between us was still there. The only thing missing was Keith. I pulled my hand away.

'I'm too drunk to drive,' I said. 'So you get to do the honours.'

Jake grinned.

* * *

The karaoke bar was loud and rowdy. There were no parking spaces, so Jake parked the truck on the side of the road. The night air was muggy out here by the lake. Each time the door opened, the music blared. A woman was singing a very bad rendition of a Gretchen Wilson tune. Men were lined up at the bar, holding down stools while they eyed the women walking back and forth. Waitresses slid bottles of beer across tables and flirted with customers. The DJ was drinking just as fast as he was playing songs.

We slid into a table at the corner next to the stage. The speaker was right in front of us and so talking was virtually impossible. I called for a Bud Light and the waitress slid them down to us like the professional she was. Jake watched me the whole time he drank his. I knew he was looking, and so I carefully kept my eyes on the singer.

77

A Toby Keith song came next. Jake slid his hand across my thigh. My eyes met his, but he didn't move his hand.

By the time I had finished the beer, caution had disappeared. I took his hand and led him to the dance floor. The grace I had first seen in him was evident out there among the two-steppers. He spun me effortlessly. Every time he pulled me back towards him, we were a little closer. By the time the song was over, we were in each other's arms.

The next song was a slow one. Jake and I didn't notice the singer at all. We were too busy enjoying the way it felt to be so close to one another. We moved in a slow waltz. Jake kissed my neck and trailed his lips along my collarbone. His lips found my ear and stayed there for a long while, kissing and singing softly along with the music. Before the song was over, his lips were on mine and I was kissing him right back.

The next number was a fast dance track. We stood back and looked at each other as the dance floor filled up. By silent agreement, we went back to the table and held hands while we watched everyone else. I occasionally looked at him, and every time I did I caught him studying me.

Another beer and I was brave enough to sing. Jake watched me as I sang, a smile on his lips. He was the one who clapped the loudest, even though I was sure I sounded just as drunk as I felt. I was surprised when Jake came up to the stage right after me. His voice was deeper than I had imagined it would be, and he was a hit with the bar, especially the ladies. I watched as they crowded around the front of the stage and looked at him with lustful eyes.

When Jake came down off the stage, he kissed me quickly on the lips.

'I'm jealous,' I admitted, and he looked at me for a long time.

'Let's go home,' he finally said.

***

I stumbled up onto the porch, laughing. I wasn't drunk enough to forget things, but I was definitely feeling good. Jake was right behind me. His laugh was genuine, hard and deep, from the belly up. He twirled me onto the wide porch and caught me right before I fell.

I wrapped my arms around his shoulders and kissed him. Jake kissed me right back, until we were both breathing hard, until my head spun from something other than the alcohol.

He asked me only one question. 'Where's the bed?'

I took him into the house. We left the door open and our clothes on the floor. I fell into the bed and Jake was immediately there beside me. His hands were everywhere. Discovering his body was like a different kind of liquor. I was drunk on him.

'My God,' he breathed. 'Look at you ...'

Jake settled above me and kissed my throat. The heat of his arousal was insistent against my thigh, but he didn't let me have it. He held himself just out of reach. I touched him everywhere and kissed every inch my lips could find. I reached for him with my hips. He chuckled against my mouth. Then he was chuckling and humming and murmuring against my nipples as I held them up to him, pushed them together so he could take both into his mouth at once.

He slid an inch of himself into me, just enough to give me a taste of what he might feel like. I tried to get him deeper but he braced himself above me. He watched as I moved under him.

'That's gorgeous,' he said. 'I love the way you try to get me inside you.'

I slid my hands down his back and grabbed his hips. He gave me that wicked smile. I pushed hard and thrust up at the same time, and was rewarded with another few inches of him. Jake laughed out loud, and I laughed right along with him.

'Please, baby,' I murmured. 'Please?'

He slowly pushed forwards. It seemed to take an eternity before he was completely inside me. Our bodies pressed tightly together. I lay very still and enjoyed the feeling of being filled by him. Jake closed his eyes and didn't move for the longest time.

'I have wanted this since the moment I saw you,' he said.

Jake started to move. I gasped with the thrill of that first gliding thrust. Hard and fast or slow and easy, it seemed everything he wanted was exactly what I wanted, too. I was wetter than I had been in recent memory, and Jake appreciated it by moving harder into me. Our hips slammed into each other. His hands tightened in my hair. I scraped my nails down his back and he cursed sweetly through gritted teeth.

Soon all the foreplay was over and we were in the middle of an all-out, hard-core fuck.

He drove me up the bed with his thrusts. I arched right back against him. The harder he gave it to me, the harder he got it. His kiss bruised my lips. I nipped at his. He pulled out and shoved me onto my belly, and was instantly on top of me, his hands in my hair as he yanked my head back. He slammed into me from behind and I could hardly catch my breath.

'You're a good fuck,' he growled into my ear.

'You're getting there,' I answered.

Jake paused in mid-stroke. He laughed out loud. 'Oh, you're going to pay for that.'

'Good. I haven't seen your best yet.'

The next thrust almost knocked me into the headboard. I braced myself hard on the mattress and pushed back against him. He thrust so hard that my elbows gave way, and I had to grab on to the headboard to keep from hitting it. Pain flashed through me as he hit bottom again and again. My legs trembled. Those finally gave way too, and he pinned me down to the bed with his weight. He thrust hard into me, driving right into that certain spot that drove me wild.

I came with a satisfied howl, but Jake didn't let up. He didn't even slow down.

'Jesus, Jake!'

'Had enough yet?'

I bit my lip. No way was I going to be the one to cry uncle. Jake slammed me hard. Surely he had to get tired soon – surely. I grabbed handfuls of the quilt under me and yelled at him, taunted him and drove his passion to an even higher pitch.

'Is that the best you got, Jake?'

Jake rolled me over onto my back. I almost toppled off the edge of the bed. He yanked me back by one leg. He lifted my legs over his shoulders and then pushed them even further back. His hands were spread wide on my thighs as he pushed my knees up to my shoulders.

Jake slammed in with one hard thrust. He pushed so deep, I could almost taste him. The pain flashed through me and I screamed aloud in surprise.

'That's what I wanted,' he growled. 'I wanted to make you fucking scream.'

He did it again. And again. Over and over, while I

clawed at his back and begged him to stop, begged him to keep going, begged him to come as deep inside me as he could.

Jake finally began to lose control. His arms trembled on either side of me. Sweat ran down his body. He threw his head back and cried out loud as he shoved as deep as he could. He throbbed inside me. The heat of him flooded me. I rocked against him. He held himself deep, until the thrill of the orgasm had passed.

Jake collapsed over me, breathing hard. 'Is that good enough?' he asked, as soon as he caught his breath.

I smiled against his skin. 'I'm going to hurt so bad tomorrow.'

'Do you mind?'

'No.'

Jake carefully rolled off me. He pulled me against him, even though we were both overheated and covered in a fine sheen of sweat. He kissed my forehead. 'Sleep with me,' he said.

'I just did.'

Jake laughed weakly. He closed his eyes. I watched him for a moment before I closed mine, too.

***

The next day, the phone rang. I was sitting on the couch, eating oatmeal, trying not to think and nursing the aches

83

and pains of a body that had been roughly used. Jake was sitting in the recliner and reading the newspaper. We looked at each other through the space of two rings.

'It's him,' Jake said.

'What do I say?'

'You be honest. He knows I'm here. He probably knows what we did, too.'

I blushed. Jake smiled and looked down at the newspaper, but I knew his whole attention was focused on the phone call. I answered and Keith's voice came over the line.

'Did you two have fun?' he asked, and I was silent for one beat too long. I started to say something, but Keith cut me off. 'It's all right. I sent him there.'

I closed my eyes. 'Why did you do that?'

Keith sighed. 'Because I realised after you left that we really had reached a crossroads. I realised you and I had found something that we might never be able to compromise on. But I knew that you and Jake thought along the same lines.'

There was actual pain in my chest as I listened to the sadness in Keith's words.

'We're over?' I asked, though I already knew.

'I think we are,' Keith said gently.

I started to cry. 'I'm sorry, Keith. It's not about you. It's about me, I think.'

I could hear Keith's smile. 'Don't cry over guilt, baby.

You haven't done anything wrong. You can't make a heart feel what it just doesn't feel, you know?'

'I love you, Keith.'

'I know. And I love you, too. That's what makes this so hard.'

We sat in silence for a few moments. Jake had put down the newspaper and was watching me intently, but he didn't make any move to get up and come to me. He wasn't going to interfere.

'I have it easier than you,' Keith said suddenly.

'What do you mean?'

'It's easier for me, because I know Jake will take care of you.'

That was why he had sent Jake. He knew this was coming, and he wanted me to be OK once it did. Suddenly I realised that he really did mean what he said – that it wasn't about not caring. It was about caring so much that he wanted the best things for me, no matter what those things might be.

'I wish you had someone there with you,' I said slowly, realising that I really did mean it. 'You deserve someone. I would give anything to know you will be OK.'

Keith cleared his throat. 'I will be OK. I promise you that. I've never broken a promise to you, have I?'

I smiled. 'Never.'

'Now listen to me, baby. I think there's a man around there somewhere who needs some attention. I'm willing to bet he's scared to death right now, but he's trying hard not to show it. You need to let him know I'm not a threat. You understand?'

That set off a fresh round of tears. Had I ever known someone so selfless?

'Yes.'

'I'll see you both when you come back to town.'

'Will you?'

Keith laughed, and though I could hear the tears, I knew it was genuine. 'Absolutely.'

I said goodbye and hung up the phone. Jake looked at me from the recliner. He hadn't moved and he looked calm, but a storm was brewing in his eyes. I stood up and walked slowly to him. I took his hand in mine, and he squeezed hard enough to hurt.

'Is he all right?' Jake asked.

'He will be.'

'Are you OK?' he asked, though we both knew I wasn't.

I looked into his eyes and offered the one thing that I knew would make us both feel better. 'Take me to bed,' I said, and Jake smiled.

Falling
Charlotte Stein

I suppose I'll be a fallen woman, soon. Of course everything seems respectable on the surface – he takes me out to tea and he tells my father there's a chaperone, you know. There even is a chaperone, though mostly she seems to sort of fade away once we're sat together in some secluded corner.

I suspect she's a friend. A mistress, perhaps, though whenever I think of the word it sounds almost unbearably exotic. Too exotic for the likes of me, little prim Lyds Alcott, in my flowery dresses and cardigans and sensible shoes. I look so out of place in the restaurants he takes me to, like a plain daisy amidst the roses. Or perhaps something better than roses. Some flower I can't even imagine, rich and vivid with colour and scent, petals too thick and the heart of it pulsing and pulsing.

This is how his world seems to me, though I don't say so. I don't say anything at all, really, because I don't want him to know how small and gauche I am inside. How I want to finger the fur of his suits and how I marvel at the littlest thing he does, like the way he smokes. He smokes as though he's done it for a thousand years, effortlessly, in rich curling plumes that emerge from between his parted lips in ways I've never seen before.

All I have are memories of sixth form, so close and yet so far away, girls lined up behind the greenhouse, plucking at their cheap little cigarettes. Spitting out puffs of smoke as though it were the height of sophistication, unaware of this secret world of champagne in shallow, narrow-stemmed glasses and jewels dripping off people like marvellous fruits, and Harrow, Harrow gazing at me with his still blue eyes.

'Would you care for another, Lyds darling?' he asks, but I know why. He isn't being polite. He wants me to have another so by the time we retire to the hotel room he's illicitly gotten for us I'll be half drunk.

That is the way men of ill repute persuade naive young girls to part with their modesty. It's the way naive young girls go from being such to being mistresses or fallen women or whatever it is you want to call it. But he should really know, funnily enough, that these terms do not scare me. In fact, I find myself welcoming them, I find myself just waiting for them to come, for the time I will no longer be Lyds Alcott and can at last become Lydia.

Perfect, poised Lydia, hard-hearted mistress of the exceedingly rich and titled Henry Harrow. She wouldn't care whether Harrow loved her or not. She wouldn't care about the path she finds herself on, so lost and alone in a world that can never be the way she longs for it to be.

The world is cold and hard and brutal, and dressing up in all the jewels and flowers in the world won't change that.

'Should we retire?' he asks, and I say yes. It's time to retire.

We go up to our room and I slip a hand over his arm when he offers. He probably thinks I need support and I suppose in one way I do. I'm about to lose my virginity and even when I squint at that fact hard-heartedly, it's still a daunting prospect.

His thirty-eight seems very far from my eighteen, suddenly, and I find myself thinking of all the things he must have done in his long life. All the strange things with women far more worldly than me, that all appear behind my eyes as a succession of contorted limbs and sliding, slippery bodies. Everything is golden in these imaginings and yet somehow still nightmarish, and when we get to the room and he slips out of his jacket, I'm suddenly afraid.

Of course I understand the practicalities of the thing. He's going to take off all my clothes, and then all of his clothes, and then he's going to climb on top of me and push his great thing into my body. And it *is* a great thing, too, because I saw it once when he was changing, through those modern underthings of his and with the suspenders clipped to his socks down below – so funny, somehow.

Though it's not really so funny now. I go to the bathroom and stand in there for ages, unsure as to whether I should take my dress off or not. He hasn't said anything but then again he so rarely does. He's not a big talker, Harrow. The most I can remember him saying to me when we met in the gallery was 'Well, what are you doing here?' As though he could hardly comprehend a single girl, alone, looking at the paintings.

I decide to go back out again in my dress. If he wants me to take it off he can say so, though when I do actually find myself in the bedroom with him something seems not quite right. The room is lovely – of course it is – with a set of double doors that go out onto a balcony, you know, and he's opened one of them so the night air can come in a bit.

It's almost … I don't know. Romantic, I suppose. Though it seems like a silly word. Especially as he's laid in bed just waiting for me, in his pyjamas of all things. He's not even reading the paper or looking over some work thing, either, as I had expected. He's just gazing at me and I feel awkward, suddenly, though not in the way I had thought I would.

It's a warm awkwardness. Like lying in the sun by a riverbank, on a summer's day – though I can't say what's awkward about that.

'Come on then, Lyds,' he says and pats the bed beside him, as though it's nothing. As though I'm just a big silly and, oh, it makes such a feeling engulf me. It rushes through me so thick and hard I can't help blurting out: 'Aren't you going to take my clothes off, first?'

Even though saying something like that is just ridiculous. He even laughs and he so rarely laughs. My face burns red to hear it.

'No,' he says, and that's even worse somehow. What does he mean, no? Why does he sound so incredulous, suddenly – and he's still smiling, too. 'Though you might be a touch more comfortable in your nightie, don't you think?'

It comes to me in a shameful flash, then. I haven't brought a nightie. I didn't think I'd need one and, oh no, I've made some sort of fatal error. I've cast myself as some sort of loose and very naked woman before he's even made me one, though I suppose he might be joking. Is he joking?

His expression softens and he says, 'Come on now, old thing.'

Which is very strange indeed, because in actual fact I've

never felt younger. I go to the bed and climb in, with my dress still on and my stockings still on and my hair still done – though it's not as though I have it all curled and set the way most of the women around here do – and he puts an arm around me, almost like a friend would.

And then he kisses me, in a way a friend definitely wouldn't.

Of course he's kissed me before. I didn't expect him to at all – when he first invited me to the gallery's new exhibit I thought he meant as a kindly patron, you know. I didn't expect him to pull me to him and press his mouth against mine with a good deal more passion than any of those sixth-form boys ever did.

But it's different now, because we're in bed together and this is it. This is what he's been angling for all of these months, in all of those almost-chaste kisses in his car outside my house, and his polite conversations with my father, and his little presents of the kind I'm sure many mistresses receive. Little trinkets, pairs of shoes. Books, hundreds of books.

'Lydia,' he says, as he kisses my throat, and I think *at last*. At last I'm not 'dear' or 'darling' or 'old thing' or 'Lyds'. I am Lydia, and he has his big hands on my waist and his body almost pressed against mine and I've no idea what I'm doing.

Should I unbutton his pyjamas? I'm not sure that's the done thing, but, oh, I can't help wondering what he really looks like, underneath. I think he's hairy, because I can sometimes see the hair over his undershirt. And I know he has a broad chest, because it fills out every suit he wears.

But when I go to touch him, he pushes my hands away and says, 'No, no, darling,' which quite puts me out of sorts. I hardly know what to think now, and even more so when he clasps my breast quite suddenly, through my dress, and says, 'You're very beautiful, Lydia.'

What on earth is he talking about? I'm not very beautiful at all. I'm sort of ordinary and mousy, even if those words sound very convincing in his low, chocolatey voice. He has a lovely voice really, a voice that makes me shiver, and, here, in the darkness, it sounds even better.

I feel certain he's about to tell me how he's going to make love to me now. And I suppose, in a way, he does just that. He slides a hand down over my body, slow and syrupy, and when he gets to the waiting place between my legs – the place where I'm burning, just absolutely burning – he says, quite matter-of-factly, 'Have you ever touched yourself?'

I have no idea why. I don't know what he means at all, though I try to force myself to say yes. Yes, of course I have. Hasn't everybody? But instead I have to go with no, because what if he asks me a more detailed question? All I could say is *Once, I thought of you so much I pressed something between my legs hard enough to hurt.*

It doesn't seem like much of anything, really.

'Never here?' he asks, and then he strokes me just once through all of that material, and I can't answer. It feels as though I'm huge down there. As though I've grown three sizes.

'Shhh,' he says, and this time I know why. I'm all … I don't know what I am. He pushes a hand underneath the material of my knickers and the whatever-it-is gets worse, because I'm wet and he can tell. He strokes through the folds of my sex and when he does he makes a little satisfied sighing sound, as though he's not Harrow at all any more. He's someone else, someone who talks a lot and breathes out in this soft, pleasurable sort of way, while his fingers circle my little bud.

I don't mind admitting: it feels like dying. I can't help bucking up into his working hand, even though I've always had a very clear picture of how I would behave in these sorts of situations. Rigid, I thought, and sort of indifferent, like a doll he'd decided to make love to instead of a real person.

But I don't feel like a doll now. I'm squirming, actually squirming. He says, 'Ah yes, my lovely Lydia,' and I don't know what to think, I'm not sure how to react, I'm clutching at his arm and there's this really deep, full sensation building between my legs.

One that gets bigger when I move and bigger yet when I don't, until I'm sure I'm about to die.

Only I can't do that, because if I do he will undoubtedly tell everyone. I can just see him now, stood there at my funeral like a posh paperweight, nodding sagely when someone asks him how it happened.

Well, he'll say. *It was a devilish business. I touched her quim with my hand and she dissolved into a fine paste. Quite awful, really. But what can you do about these fallen women?*

I don't know. I don't know. I only know that it feels blissful, and sort of like I'm exploding, and then, oh then, oh no, he does it with his mouth *as well* as his hand. That can't be right, can it? I swear to you, God, I don't like it one little tiny bit.

Even in all the places where I do. Like behind my knees, where everything's gone all fizzy and tingly. And low down in my stomach, where it pulses the moment he kisses me just there. Right in the place he had his finger, a moment ago.

I think it's called a clim or a clat or something like it – well, that's its real name, at least – but in truth it just feels like a little bead, and the more he kisses over it the bigger those pulses get. The more my body thrums and thrums and wants out of its own skin, until he puts a hand on my thigh and demands I stay still.

He has to concentrate, I suppose, because it's all very complicated when you really think about it. The way my knickers are still bunched and twisted between my legs, one side of them pulled away so he can get at me. The way he's using his fingers to spread me open, so he can kiss me and lick me all around that little hard shape, that little nothing that I've never actually thought about until right now.

I mean, I knew it was there. I knew there was *some-thing* there. But it's different when someone's running a soft, wet tongue over it, so slippery and good. It forces me to do something worse than move around and make a nuisance of myself – a sound comes out of my mouth, as loud as a firework in this snooty little room.

But he doesn't seem to mind that half so much as he minded the squirming. He doesn't pop his head up and tell me to be quiet, in a tone as firm as his hand on my thigh. He doesn't even jostle me, or slow the pace of the thing he's doing.

Instead, he licks harder. Faster.

And now I think I'm really going to die. This is it. I'm done for. He's too good at this – whatever this is – and my end is coming, even if it's the kind of end I've often dreamed of, rather than the one I'd assumed would come to me, walking in here.

It's a good end, I think. A dying-of-pleasure sort of end – like the ones the girls in the sixth-form toilets frequently talk about. They chatter about 'mind-blowing' and 'awe-inspiring', though really I don't think they have any idea what they're talking about.

Because my mind doesn't go away anywhere, and my awe isn't inspired. Instead, I think of the roller coaster at Blackpool, the one that makes you go up and down and up and down and when you get off you feel all jangled – and that's what it's like. These waves go up and down inside my body, and I can't seem to breathe, and I go all tense, even though I'm sure I should be relaxing into it, or something.

And then after I feel sort of like a lunatic, because I'm shaky and not in full control of myself and he's just staring down at me with his strange, still eyes. Everything about Harrow is so perfectly still, all of the time – so composed.

Why am I not composed? I can't even be composed now, in the middle of sex.

'Pleasant?' he asks, and I think he means the thing that just happened. As in: *Was it pleasant?* But that seems daft, somehow, because of *course* it was pleasant. You'd have to be a fool to think it might be otherwise, and Harrow is no fool.

So why is he asking? Is this the one area in which he is not fully aware, fully in control, fully everything? I can't imagine it is and yet he's still looking down at me, waiting and waiting for me to say yes.

It makes me nervous. But it makes me something else, too. Something brilliant, I reckon – like a girl worthy of the name *Lydia*.

'Perfect,' I say, and for once I don't feel as though I've said the wrong thing. I feel relaxed, and at ease, and still stuffed full of all of those bizarre roller-coaster sensations. They bolster me as he leans forwards and slides his hands back up my thighs, to catch on the elastic of my underwear and drag them all the way down and off.

Of course, I know how I should feel at that point. Naked and exposed and rude. Like those bathroom girls, flashing each other when they think no one's looking.

But I don't. I want him to see. I want him to see how wet I've gotten – because I have. I can feel it. It's all over my thighs and between the cheeks of my arse, but when he looks me over – skirt hiked up, cheeks flushed, sex all slippery – he doesn't look disapproving or mortified. His eyes are heavy-lidded, instead, and when he speaks his voice is hoarse.

I think that's a good thing. In fact I know it's a good thing, because when he unbuttons his pyjama bottoms and takes them off, I can see his prick pressing against his underwear. I can see how big it is, and how stiff – though I don't get the full benefit of it until he's completely naked, lying next to me on the bed.

And even then I'm not entirely sure what to think. He's very big all over, though of course I knew that already. He used to row back when he was at university and, even if he hadn't, I know he would have been an imposing man.

It's the broad shoulders, I think, and the long legs. And maybe also his chest, which is all covered in rough hair and sort of like a barrel. Though none of these things adequately explain why I can't seem to stop looking at him, because after a long moment I realise that's all I've been doing – just staring at him everywhere, like a maniac.

It's a good thing, really, that he doesn't seem to mind. He just unbuttons my dress while I carry on trying not to look at him, and then when I get to his prick all thick and jutting up at me like a fist, he takes off my stockings, too.

It's all very easily done, because of course my attention is elsewhere. My attention is on this urge that's in me to reach down and touch him in almost the exact way he touched me.

I mean, wouldn't he like it, if I did? He probably would. Most men like it, or so I've heard. The bathroom girls are always talking about hand jobs, and I know that they don't mean arts and crafts projects.

They mean – you know. Giving a man *pleasure* with your *hand*. And now that I've looked at the thing I can see how someone could go about it – just stroke it up and down, or maybe rub it around the head a little, in all the places he looks slick and about ready to burst.

Only the thing is, when I actually do it – when I dare to reach out a hand and squeeze him, greedily – he doesn't force me to carry on or grab the back of my head and make me suck on it, the way some of the girls said men do. He makes a soft sighing sound, instead, and then after a second says: 'Wouldn't you rather I make love to you?'

It's the funniest thing. I really didn't think he'd ask. I just thought he'd grab me and do it all over me, and when he doesn't I am suddenly mired in indecision. This is the choice, I know. The choice between being a Good Girl or being a Bad One.

But I say yes anyway, because I want him, oh, I want him. I want him all over me and under me and inside me, with his mouth so usually cool and soft, now hot and fierce and hard. I almost flinch away from the feel of it, but not quite, not quite.

He's too lovely to flinch away from. He's too different, right now – like a great, unchained beast. And if I were to flinch away I think he might draw back into himself, into that cool, still place, and I don't want him to.

I *like* it when he pins my wrists above my head. I like it when he sinks his teeth into the flesh of my breasts, making circles around the nipples that I'm sure will still be there tomorrow. Little bracelets all over me, little reminders of this new person he's become.

It's so strange – I thought *I* would be the one to turn into someone else. But he's the one who digs his fingers into my hip, and makes chains of bruises all over me.

He's the one who breathes shakily when his prick slides through my spread folds, seeking the hollow of my sex.

And the moment he finds it, the moment he's ready to thrust in and make me wicked for ever, he pauses. As though doing this – it's one step too far. It's too much. He needs to know first if I can bear it.

'Do you want me to?' he asks, and I can't help it. I shove down on him, hard, in place of all the words I can't say. My body just says them for me in one long frantic push and shove, until he's buried to the hilt in my aching sex.

But he still doesn't move. He keeps deathly still, hands still tight around my wrists, breath so hot and sultry on my upturned face. And then after the longest, most agonising moment in history he finally rolls his hips – just once.

But oh, so good. So slippery, so slick, and the feel of him spreading me open ... I have to clench tightly around him, just to chase the feeling it provokes. To get a little bit more of that strange solidity, filling me. It's almost like ... almost like biting down hard to push away the ache in your gums, and I don't know, I don't know.

It's too much. It's not enough. I'm so hot I'm sure I can feel my skin blistering, but I can't move away. I don't want to. He's above me, rocking slowly, and he looks like that new person again – the different one that I've never met before and can hardly bear to look at.

101

His eyes are hazy and his lips are parted, and when he does make words they're very far from glacial. They're the filthiest, rudest things I've ever heard, and they move through me as swiftly and as gloriously as the feel of his quickening thrusts do.

'You've got the hottest, sweetest cunt,' he says, and I go red for *hottest* and redder yet for *sweetest* and then practically purple for *cunt*.

I think that feeling is starting up in me, again. And it gets worse when he tells me how slick I feel, how tight around his *cock*, how beautiful I look spread out for him like this. 'My lovely Lydia,' he says, and I can't help reaching up to kiss him then. It's awkward with my hands still pinned and I'm not sure I've ever done it off my own bat before, but I try anyway.

Because I want to give him something back, for all of this. I never give him anything back – I realise that now. I always think about things a certain way, or imagine that I'm just a game to him, just a toy. But it isn't like I'm a toy, right at this moment.

It's like I'm Lydia, his lover. And when he asks me to tell him how it feels, how much I like it like this, like this, like this, I find I can tell him. 'There,' I tell him, 'right there, do it there.'

Only I don't say 'do it'. I say 'fuck'. 'Fuck me there.'

And he does. He grips my hip hard and fucks right into my cunt, so rough I'm sure it should hurt. But it just gets sweeter and sweeter instead, all of these feelings bubbling up inside me and right out of my mouth.

'Oh God, that's so good,' I tell him, but I don't do it in a voice that sounds like my own. I do it in this high, tight, wavering sort of thing, and I press my face to his at the same time. Me – the girl who never so much as dared to take his arm, without him giving the say-so first.

But I don't need say-so right now. My body's in charge, electrified by the feel of him sliding all over me and inside me. The hand he's got over my wrists goes to my hair, suddenly, gets a fistful of it and squeezes tight as his mouth moves against my ear. 'Yes,' he says. 'Yes, tell me how much you want it. Tell me you love me.'

It's the first time I've ever heard him say that word. Though happily, it's also the first time I've ever been brave enough to answer him in kind.

'I do,' I say, in that strange tight voice. 'Oh God, I do.'

And it's true. It is. I may have fallen, but the falling has been into something else entirely – something I didn't expect. I thought of hell, of disapproving looks, of all things terrible and wicked. But this isn't like that at all.

It's like drowning in pleasure. It's like falling into *him*. My strange, cold Harrow, who has somehow turned into a different creature altogether before my very eyes – one who moans my name as that bursting thing overtakes him, too.

And I feel him – hot and slippery inside me. Hips jerking, eyes bright and dark with it, at the same time. It's almost as though he passes it along to me, that electric, white-hot sensation, and I devour it greedily.

I'm still greedy with it now, after it's all done. And I think he knows it, when he looks down at me – but that's OK. I know it too.

I can never go back and, in all honesty, I don't want to. I am a fallen woman, now, and oh, it's bliss.

Something Twisted This Way Comes
Kyoko Church

It was a dark time for him. And titillating. Dark and titillating.

He hadn't thought the two qualities could be so exquisitely combined. Or if he had, it was just an inkling he'd only known somewhere in the recesses of his mind, on the edges of his fantasies. But it was there. The chocolate and peanut butter of sexual dysfunction.

He would always remember that time. Those three weeks when he couldn't do anything. Couldn't work, couldn't sleep, couldn't eat. Couldn't do anything but think about her. Looking back he realised something. What made her, what gave her power, was what she knew. That in the human psyche there is no such thing as truth, only perspective. She understood that a person can have a secret, something he thinks is ugly. So he hides it from view, tucks it away, only visits it in secret, on weekends, and then only to torture himself, like picking at a scab. But she saw the glimmer of it. So she plucked it out, dusted it off. Turned it a hair to the left. And stood back for him to see. Waited for him to realise: the thing he most hated, he could actually love.

***

He met her innocently enough. No, that's not true. Perhaps an outside observer could have thought it was innocent. But he was not innocent. He'd been looking at some, er, pictures, at his desk at work. So he was hard. He was hard in the elevator when she stepped on, on his way to take some pressure off, taking the elevator to a more secluded bathroom on the top floor of his office building.

She stepped on, all business, tailored suit but killer heels, auburn hair swept up in a surprisingly old-fashioned chignon in contrast to the rest of her look. She was not the kind of woman he was normally attracted to. He usually went for the more petite, blonde type. She was all curves, very Marilyn Monroe, but with that hair the colour of fire. Embarrassingly, the word 'va-va-voom' ran through his head.

She looked at him. She assessed him. Sized him up.

106

Her eyes scoured him up and down, everything from his average clothes, his average shoes, his slightly balding average hair. The wedding band on his finger. The bulge in the front of his pants.

He glanced again at those heels, open-toed with her pretty red nails peeping out of the top. She caught him looking and he blushed. They exchanged not a single word. But then she smiled at him. A slow, sly smile. He saw a light go on in her eyes and in an instant he understood that she knew him. She saw what he was exactly.

'Email me,' she said, handing him a card. Then she stepped off the elevator, and was gone.

***

He emailed her the next day. Was he ever not going to? She told him to come up to her office on the 42nd floor.

When he got there, she was stretched out on the leather sofa beneath the large picture window that looked out high over the city. Her feet were up, her heels, different ones today, black patent, were on the floor. She was wearing dress pants but her feet were bare. Again, those red toenails.

'Have a seat,' she said, indicating the sofa beside her.

He settled uncomfortably at the other end, not knowing where to look or how to position his body. She chuckled. 'A little closer, silly,' she said, lifting her foot up, offering it to him as he moved closer. He blushed but took it, gently. Her foot was surprisingly small and slender, the skin pale so the red toenails stood out sharply. He began to massage slowly.

'Wait a second.' He looked up. 'Turn to me a little,' she said. 'That's right, now lift your knee up onto the couch.' He did so and jumped as she placed her other foot gently but firmly against his crotch. 'Keep rubbing,' she commanded, gesturing at the foot in his hand. 'I just want to make sure you're not getting excited.' Fire exploded in his face. He looked away from her, at her foot, then looked away from that.

She laughed. 'It's OK,' she cooed. 'I know you like my feet. And I do need a foot rub right now. So you rub them.' He hesitated. 'Do it,' she said, not laughing now. 'But I just need to make sure you're not being a disgusting pervert and getting all excited about my pretty feet. This foot rub is supposed to be for me.'

He rubbed, obediently trying to clear his mind, trying to think of anything but her slim foot in his hands. But there was also the pressure of her other foot against him. And then she started making little noises. Little whimpers, groans of pleasure. 'Mmm, that's right,' she purred. 'Ooo, right there, that feels so good.' He was helpless. He sat helplessly rubbing, while his cock grew with a mind of its own.

'Oh my God, what is going on?' She looked at him.

'I can feel you, you know,' she said, wiggling her toes against his stiffness, only worsening matters. 'God, what horny little thoughts are going through your head right now? Was it the noises I was making?' she chided. 'I was only enjoying the foot rub! You weren't thinking that's what I sound like when I fuck, were you?' He stared into his lap, unable to respond. 'Well, if you are going to act like a horny little dog, then that's how I'm going to have to treat you.'

This was how it was that he found himself, a grown man, a professional, an architect, on all fours on the floor in front of this goddess, humping her foot like some kind of human lapdog.

And even though she didn't make it easy for him by doing things like swinging her foot away, complaining that he was going too fast, laughing, forcing him to keep all four limbs on the ground, to not use his hands, even still his little problem reared its ugly head.

He spurted, hips helplessly bucking, after two minutes.

He knelt in front of her and braced himself. He steeled himself against the familiar onslaught of feeling – frustration, anger, shame – that always raged through him like a firestorm, burning through everything in its path. But instead of the usual reactions of disappointment, pity, anger or worse, the yawning silence, pregnant with judgements and unspoken resentment, there was something different.

109

Giggling. Like tinsel. Like glasses chinking together, crystal laughter.

'My, my, my, we are the eager little beaver, aren't we?'

Heat rose; he could hear the blood pump through the vessels in his head.

'That's OK, sweetie,' she said and she leaned over, put her lips right next to his ear, so he could feel her breath on his skin. 'Mistress has all sorts of ways to deal with a horny little boy like you,' she whispered.

Suddenly, he realised he was hard again. Harder than he had been the first time.

There was shame. But no anger. There was humiliation. But no frustration.

Pure humiliation. Not blazing, like the white-hot heat of the firestorm of his secret torment, but rolling in slowly, like molasses, covering him, turning his insides liquid, enveloping him in a mass of humility, shrinking him down, making him want to place his hard, needy little cock before her in an act of complete submission.

There it was. Just like that. Turned a hair to the left. His torment died. His kink was born.

***

In the first few texts and emails they exchanged she asked him questions. So many questions. He loved answering them but he could barely keep up. The questions kept coming, more and more. There were some simple ones: where, when, how often. Questions about habits with his wife, did he like this, was he turned on by that. But then came more difficult, compelling questions. Like, why. Why did he like what he did? Where did it come from? And finally, what books did he like? What TV shows did he watch? Who did he vote for in the 2008 election? Her desire to learn about him was voracious, like she was eating him alive. He felt like that. Or like in answering her, he was ripping himself open and laying his insides out for her to casually peruse and then choose something to examine.

He dutifully responded to it all.

***

And then she named him. His name was not Paul. But she named him SubPaul. He could not help but wonder if it was because it sounded like 'sub par'.

***

After lunch one day she called him in his office.

'I'm going to send you an email,' she said, the sultry tones of her voice coming through the phone like ribbons of silk weaving around his body. 'When you get it, don't open it. You are not allowed to open it until you are ready to go home.'

111

The email came through. He looked at it sitting there in his inbox, subject line '**For Your Drive**', in its bold print, indicating it was unread, the darkness of the lettering making it appear so much more intense than the other pathetic emails beneath it and eventually above it.

He glanced at the clock: 1.35. He had almost four hours until it would be appropriate, usual for him to leave. Maybe he could squeeze it to three and a half. The hours stretched out like a long road in front of him. It was torture wondering what the message said, being semi-hard over words he hadn't even read yet. How was he going to sit for all that time without reading it? What did it say?

***

From: MistressD
To: SubPaul
SUBJECT: FOR YOUR DRIVE

Hi! This email is for your drive home. If you have opened it before then, stop, close this up. Open it back up when you are about to drive home. Put it away. Now.

OK. Are you alone now? Good boy. Have you been thinking about me? Of course you have. You're always thinking about me, aren't you? I've taken up residence in that naughty little brain of yours.

I have to address the fact that your wife doesn't go down on you. Have you wondered why I haven't commented on that in our emails? Did you think I hadn't noticed or maybe it wasn't important to me? Oh no. No, no, no. I took very keen notice of that. I have thought about that. A LOT. Because here's something you should know about me. I LOVE to suck cock. I fucking love it. The power. I really get off on the power of it. I know that if I had my lips and tongue anywhere near your cock right now I would have complete control over you. Total.

So, Mr I-haven't-had-a-blow-job-in-20-years, when I get my hands on you again I'm going to strip you down, sit you on a chair, cuff your hands behind your back and start licking. That spot. You know that spot? Oh yes, the one just under your head, that sensitive spot that you told me you couldn't touch because it gets you there too quickly? Aw, poor baby. Too fucking bad. I like that spot. I would flick and tongue and kiss and suck that spot until you were a pleading, begging, weeping, sopping fucking mess. Don't you dare come in my face. I mean, Mistress loves come, but I don't want it yet.

You fucking hold it back, slut.

Now. Put your phone away. Start your car. And think about this email the whole way home. Try subtly to get Wifey to fuck you tonight. Report back to me in the morning.

Kisses!

***

Oh. God.

Oh God. Ohgodohgodohgodohgod.

Like a zombie he turned the keys in the ignition. He started the engine. His cock was so hard he could feel the vibrations of the motor right through his body. Her words ran through his brain. He could see himself, in her office, strapped to her chair, helpless with her tongue on his trigger and her ordering him not to explode. *Don't you dare come in my face.* Oh God. *You fucking hold it back, slut.* Oh fuck.

His cock gave one hard pulse. And then the combination of his pants pressing down on his stiff flesh, the vibrations from the car engine and, mostly, her words whirling around in his head sent pressure through his body it was helpless to combat. He swallowed hard, let out a strangled cry and released in one large spurt.

***

'You *what*?' She giggled uncontrollably. 'You actually came *in your pants*?'

He stood before her in her office the next day, reporting, as she requested, head down, again cheeks aflame.

'Oh my God, how old are you? You're acting like a horny teenager!' She walked around her desk over to him. She was more casual today, in a light-grey sweater dress that clung to her curves in all the right places. Her fiery hair was down and loose, cascading in waves around her face as she smiled and tsked her disapproval at him. 'I knew I had my work cut out for me with you.' She lifted his chin with her finger. 'But even I didn't think you were *this* bad.' His heart pounded. She gently placed her hand on the side of his face and stared in his eyes like she was searching for something, like she was considering a choice or trying to solve a puzzle. Then she blinked.

'You need some extra work,' she said. 'Some, um, let's call it therapy. Desensitisation. Yes, that's it!'

He began to say something, to protest somehow, even though he wasn't really sure what she meant. But she wouldn't let him speak. 'SubPaul, this is for your own good,' she chastised. 'I mean, how is your wife ever going to have any pleasure if you keep coming like a horny

115

little boy after two minutes! Or if you don't even make it into her cunt.' Oh God. The wave of humiliation was back. He felt it in his gut, deep down, hot, big in his gut and radiating out, making the edges of his body tingle. 'Coming in your pants,' she sighed. 'I mean, really!' She put a hand on her hip and stood back, still staring at him.

'Close the door,' she commanded. He obeyed.

'So here's what we're going to do,' she said. 'You obviously get very excited about the idea of my mouth on your cock.' She licked her lips. His heart skipped a beat.

She knelt in front of him and began unbuckling his pants. His hands flew to protect himself but her head snapped back and her eyes pierced him, even from her position below.

'Don't. Fucking. Move.'

He swallowed hard and obeyed, forcing his hands to hang at his sides.

When she pulled his pants and his shorts down his cock sprang out, stiff already from just her words and her position in front of him. God. His heart continued pounding its thunderous rhythm in his head. He stared up at the ceiling, searching for a way to calm down.

'Now don't look up there, look at me,' she said, 'and keep looking.' He nodded and complied. Her eyes were no longer teasing and giggly. Now they were stern.

Serious. 'Listen to what I'm telling you.' He watched her mouth move. She'd painted her lips a bright red today, perhaps to contrast her grey dress. She put that red mouth right next to his swollen member. 'You need to stop thinking about me putting my mouth on your little dick.' She kept staring into his eyes. He could feel her hot breath on him. It was crazy, so humiliating, but he could feel every puff of hot air as her words escaped her lips, each one sending waves of sensation through his cock, making it pulse and throb. 'I know you never get head. Aw, that makes it difficult, doesn't it?' Suddenly her eyes changed. Soft now, sympathetic. 'It's OK, sweetie. Mistress knows.' His insides turned to liquid. His knees mush. 'But for your own good, you need to stop. OK?' She looked at his cock. He started trembling but he didn't dare move. She made her mouth into an O and put it a sliver, a hair away from the tip, and looked up at him again. 'Unh unh,' she sang. She pulled away slightly so her lips wouldn't touch him as she said, 'Stop thinking about me sucking you.'

Then she put out her tongue, put it on the base of his trembling cock, and licked one long soft but firm, wet lick from the base all the way up to the tip, dragging that gorgeous tongue across every horny, sensitive fibre of his being. When she got to the tip, he exploded.

She let him. She put her hands on his bucking hips and held her tongue there as his cock convulsed and

117

gushed, pulsing out its creamy disgrace. She caught it all on her tongue and then she stood.

She put a hand on either side of his face, tilted his head back slightly and put her lips to his as if in a kiss. He obediently opened his lips to her as she deposited his still-warm come in his own mouth. She licked, pursed her lips and stepped back.

'Certainly you don't expect *me* to clean up after you.' She smiled. 'Swallow your own fucking come.'

She turned on her heel and left.

* * *

It was not completely true to say he couldn't work. He couldn't – he sat at his desk, in his office, gazing unseeingly at his blank computer screen, a million miles away, for hours. So he couldn't. Until he could.

Until he had an idea. And his ideas, like his cock, were not controllable, would pop up at inconvenient times and demand attention. Like one night, in the wee hours, when he suddenly woke and sat straight up in bed, gasping. He could see the building, the plans, see all of the lines, curves, intersections everything before him. His brain seemed to be working on autopilot, calculating the structure, envisioning how the light would come through. He glanced at the clock – 3.32 – and at his sleeping wife and briefly considered trying to go back to sleep. He almost heard his idea, like a person, like Her, laughing at him. Just try and ignore me! it seemed to say. The voice, Her voice, propelled him out of bed.

He walked into his darkened home office, looked at his drawing board. At home he still went old school with pencil and paper. The prospect of transcribing everything from his brain to the waiting blank paper simultaneously exhausted and exhilarated him. He envisioned himself reaching for his brain, through his ear, pulling it out and pitching it at that board, splat! Then watching as all his ideas gelled into drawings, all his best stuff emerging, like wheat from chaff.

He worked feverishly until morning.

***

Standing on the stairs to the library entrance, he stopped, looked up at the doors and took in a deep breath. He took out his phone and reread her email. The one with the subject line: 'Consequences'. That email was the reason he was there.

He didn't want to be there. A part of him, something in his head, was screaming at him to please turn around, get back in his car and go home to his wife. But it was not a request. She was very clear. There were consequences for his failure at their first therapy session, as she referred to it. He had to learn.

119

So he was at the library. Her orders were: go into the library, go to the non-fiction section, go to the librarian at the information desk and ask her for help. Because apparently he needed it.

He had to ask for books on premature ejaculation.

He took one last breath. And walked in.

* * *

That's how their relationship went. Therapy. Consequences. More therapy.

Usually the therapy took place in her office. He would come in, usually in the morning, and report to her on his night: if he had masturbated, if his wife had consented to sex, if he was able to last long enough to let her have an orgasm. He would confess everything to her, head down, mumbling a bit, her naughty puppy.

She would giggle and laugh at his inadequacies, provoking that now familiar heat in his stomach, making it rumble like she was reaching in and messing with it, like the way she might tousle a naughty boy's hair.

Then the therapy would commence. The first time was the worst. And so also the best.

He presented her with the library books, demonstrating that he had completed her humiliating task. She lavished him with compliments, praised him, told him she was

120

happy that at least he was able to do this, making up for his lack of performance in therapy.

Then she put the books aside. 'I have my own methods,' she said. 'Come, SubPaul.' She was sitting at her desk. As he walked around the desk to her, she reached into a drawer and pulled out a pair of latex gloves and a bottle of lubricant. 'You don't have a latex allergy, do you?' she asked, smiling.

He couldn't speak. Just shook his head, no.

The familiar crystal giggle. 'Oh, that's good. Because you don't think your cock is actually worthy of my hands, do you? Maybe once you can last longer than a minute or two, then you might get my hands. But until then you only get the gloves.' She looked up at him from her chair and sighed. 'Pull your pants down, silly boy! Do I have to do everything for you?'

He quickly unbuckled and took his pants down to his knees. Watching her take the bottle of lube and pour some onto her black-gloved hand stiffened his already hardening cock.

'Now remember my instructions from last time. They haven't changed. You must watch me. You must not move. You can do that, right?' He nodded. 'Good boy!' She rubbed the substantial amount of lubricant between both gloves, put her hands together as if in prayer, and then slowly slid his hardness between her two slick gloved palms.

God! He swallowed hard and closed his eyes. 'Eyes open, darling!' she chimed. 'Forgetting the rules already? I'll let it go this time. Don't do it again.'

Slowly, oh so slowly, excruciatingly slowly, she pumped him two more times. Already he could feel his balls tense up, his seed beginning to simmer.

'Now, see how good I am to you? I am giving you a chance by going really slowly. I know you couldn't last a second if I went with any kind of normal speed.' While she spoke she switched tactics, put one smooth gloved palm on his tightened ball sac and pumped in a twisting motion with her other hand. He obediently watched and listened to her, watched his helpless cockhead pulse with purple intensity and weep pre-come. 'If you get close, you have to tell me, OK? You have to ask permission for a break. No coming without permission! That would make for some harsh consequences.'

Oh God! He was going to have to stop her already. He didn't want to say it. He couldn't bear for her to know that it was already too much. But the threat of the consequences. Oh God. Oh fuck.

'Mistress, stop!' He panted. Struggled.

'Now that wasn't very polite!' she said, continuing to stroke.

'Oh God! I'm sorry, Mistress! Please stop! Please!' She continued. 'Please, Mistress, may I have a break!'

She stopped.

He nearly fell over he was trembling so badly, straining so hard to stop himself.

'Now that's better,' she said. 'You must always remember to be polite to me. I'm trying to help you. But look at your hips. They're bucking like you're a dog or something. And what's this?' Even while she spoke without touching him, he was still desperately trying to hold his come in. But as her words came out, so too did one small drop from his dick. Not clear pre-come. But white, the colour of shame.

'Oh-ho! You let a little bit out!' And to his astonishment she was smiling. 'Do you know what that means? You let a little bit out. You started coming a little bit. But you held it back! Good for you! I'm proud of you. Now we're making some progress.' He blushed, insanely grateful for this compliment. But then her smile changed. Morphed. Then it wasn't a friendly smile. It was a little bit evil. A little bit knowing. A smile that made him tremble even more.

'But now, your little cock is going to be really horny and sensitive,' she said. And when she touched it again, he found out just how right she was. And he nearly cried.

As she slowly stroked, he almost wept from the sensitivity, the intensity, the conflict of the near painfully glorious feeling and trying to control his body, make it stop doing what it wanted so badly to do.

'Aw, poor baby!' she said as she continued her slow

stroking. 'I told you. I warned you it was going to be sensitive. That's your own body's self-imposed punishment for letting that little drop out. That's wonderful, isn't it?'

He really did cry then. Sobbed out, 'Please, Mistress, may I have another break,' as his hips bucked uncontrollably and his cock pulsed with need and struggle.

She stopped. 'Aw, of course, sweetie. Stop crying now,' she whispered gently. She looked up at him and her eyes shone brightly. 'Here,' she said. 'Let me kiss it better.' Then she took his cock with one gloved hand, cupped his balls with the other, put his whole cockhead in her glorious mouth and gave it one big, wet, passionate French kiss.

And of course. He exploded.

***

He knew it couldn't last for ever. Somehow he just knew. And in the end three weeks was what it amounted to.

One day he sat down at his laptop, opened his email and there was one from her. The subject line was 'The end comes quickly.' He actually chuckled. But he knew it was done.

It was a dark time for him. And very, intensely, insanely titillating.

But it was more.

Because for those three weeks he had never felt more alive, never more vibrant, never more connected to the world, to the air, to the trees, to other people. He felt like he caught a glimmer of how the universe fitted together, that just for a moment he could see what some people called God.

And it was because of her.

Thinking now, he changed his mind. It wasn't dark then. It was dark before. Then she came along, reached in, shuffled some things around, turned the light on and left.

The Carrot and the Stick
Chrissie Bentley

'He just walked out of the bathroom, straight over to the bed, stuck his dick in my mouth and told me he wasn't going to take it out until I told him what was wrong.'

Helen paused; I gasped. 'So what did you do?'

'I sucked him dry!' She laughed and took another drag on her cigarette. 'It had been so long, I thought I'd forgotten how to do it. But it's amazing how quickly things come back to you when they're ... shall we say, staring you in the face.'

Now it was my turn to laugh. The last time I saw Helen and Terry together, I'd have laid odds on their marriage not lasting another month. They barely spoke, they never looked at one another, and anybody who didn't know them would have said they were complete strangers, who just happened to be at a party together. Suggest they'd been married for fourteen years, and you'd have been laughed out of sight. But they had, and the sad thing was, there was a time when they couldn't keep their hands off one another.

That was a long time ago, though, and I think most of our friends knew that things had been going downhill between them for a long time. Now, however ...

Friends take sides, and I'd gravitated firmly to Helen's, not from some sense of 'all girls together', but because I was one of the first (if not *the* first) of our circle in whom she confided, around the time she and Terry hit one of the worst anniversaries any couple can attain: 'twelve months since we last had meaningful sex'. As in, sex that doesn't involve a thirty-second tumble in the middle of the night, that ends the moment the guy's shot his load.

It wasn't all Terry's fault, she assured me; the longer they were together, the harder she found it to communicate her needs as well. 'I mean, you can't just turn to your husband and say "My pussy could really use a good licking," can you? You *should* be able to, but you can't.'

I shook my head. Happily *un*married as I am, I really cannot envision being in any kind of relationship where you feel too embarrassed, shy, *whatever*, to make your physical feelings known, no matter how crude your wording may be (*come here, hun, and fuck my titties, will ya?*). At the same time, though, I've certainly had long-term boyfriends with whom it was easy to let that side of things slide a little. Well, there's always other stuff to do, isn't there? The time is never right, there's something on TV.

Terry had certainly found a way around that particular problem. And a rather arousing one at that. I wondered vaguely what he'd have done if Helen had simply moved her head to spit him out. Or maybe that was the idea, one final test to let him know exactly where he stood. Now he knows, and the only thing Helen spat out was the come shot that flooded her mouth at the end. 'But I don't think he noticed, and I had him back in there for the last few drips anyway.' A shadow crossed her face. 'I'm sorry, I'm not grossing you out, am I?'

I patted her shoulder. 'Not at all. I love it when …' I stopped as the waiter arrived at our table, but I think he'd heard all he needed to, regardless; the look he flashed at Helen told me that.

***

Helen saw it as well. 'I should have ordered the oysters in white sauce,' she said as he walked away.

'With a side dish of mayo,' I added. 'And an extra napkin.'

We were still giggling when my boyfriend, Ray, arrived. Six months had passed since he and I first met – six months, during which he had wholly uprooted his own life back east, and moved to the west coast, to be with me? Actually, no – to be closer to the bulk of his business clients. But his new-found proximity certainly hadn't hurt our own relationship; in fact, the knowledge that we could just meet up for lunch a few times a week had placed us on an even keel that our first few weeks of jet-lagged jumps had never prepared me for.

Of course, we girls both had to stifle another bout of giggling when Ray *did* order the oysters, but finally we said our goodbyes. I promised to call Helen back that evening, and jumped a cab to the gallery Ray had just purchased a partnership in. It was a downtown affair of such upmarket pretension that its very architecture almost blinded you to the engraved sign on the door that announced the various proprietors' specialties: celebrity portraits, modern landscapes and, courtesy of Ray, vintage erotica.

Vintage erotica. It really does sound kind of unsavoury, doesn't it? I mean, I've been dating Ray all this time and I still conjure up images of some seedy little man with a musty, messy back-alley store, selling dirty postcards in plain brown envelopes to furtive businessmen wearing suspenders under their suits. When, in fact, the entire operation could not be more above board.

He advertises in the best magazines, his client base swings from government officials to captains of industry – and, to even reach Ray's showroom at the gallery, you have to pass first through three other, vast, mahogany'd halls, filled with photographic art of every description. But then you pass through the heavy wine curtains that drape the rear wall, and you forget everything you saw on the way in, to lose yourself instead in a lost world of monochrome sexuality.

Three thoughts on that subject. First, our grandparents obviously weren't as prudish as we like to think. Secondly, they could teach a lot of modern 'porn stars' something about displaying the Body Beautiful. And third, they had some very strange ideas. OK, not strange, but certainly not what we'd call conventional about what is and isn't sexy. Lots of pissing, lots of pipes and cigarettes being inserted in vaginas and, if you look closely, a lot of rather ludicrous disguises – men with false Groucho noses, things like that. It's also refreshing to realise that the modern fad for ultra-skinny models is just that, a fad. The women in these photographs certainly aren't fat. But neither do they look like they might snap from one over-vigorous fuck. In other words, just normal women doing what, for them, appeared to be normal things.

'Except they weren't normal,' Ray explained. 'You have to remember, the camera itself was still a fairly recent invention; it certainly wasn't the kind of device you ran into every day. So the models in the pictures might well have been having their picture taken for the very first time – which means, there was such novelty value in it that the actual nature of the photograph was probably a very distant second to the fact that they were being photographed in the first place.'

He handed me a loose bundle of pictures that he'd obviously just received in that day's mail (yes, it is legal to send such things through the mail – in fact, much of Ray's business is conducted that way). 'These were pulled out of the basement of, believe it or not, an old church that was being renovated in Arkansas. One of the workmen found them, took them home to look through, then put them up on eBay. Luckily, he didn't have a clue what they were, didn't have a scanner, and only pulled in a few bids. I got them for $30, but I'll probably be sending him another grand by the time I've sold them.'

I looked at him blankly. 'I thought you'd already bought them?'

'I have. But one thing I learned long ago, if someone brings you something good, particularly someone in that line of work, treat them right. Because that way, if they come across anything else …' He gestured to a rather striking blow-up on the wall, a veritable triptych, showing a priest in a devil mask taking a nun from behind. 'A demolition worker in Brooklyn found the originals, got in touch, and we sold the set for five grand, gave him three hundred dollars and what do you know? The following week he sent us another batch that he'd been holding on to as a souvenir.'

I flicked through the photos in my hand, paused as Ray lay his hand on my wrist. 'Gently. These things are fragile.' I apologised and, instead, spread the pictures out on his desk. 'Another priest?'

'Priests were a popular subject. Any profession that was considered "above" that kind of behaviour. You also see a lot of well-to-do lords giving the chambermaid one. There's even a few done up to look like famous politicians and royalty.' He rummaged through a file for a moment, then pulled out a shot of a man with wild staring eyes, long unkempt hair, and his tongue lolling out of his mouth, lying prone on the floor, while a woman stood above him with a wide, gaping vagina. The caption insisted, "The Real Death of Rasputin".

'The implication ...' began Ray.

'Yes, I know what the implication is.' I smiled. 'Still, at least he died happy.'

'There was a lot of humour in pornography back then,' Ray continued. 'A lot more than you find today. Puns, wordplay. I don't know if it was a conscious attempt to lessen the shock of the actual picture, or if it was just the way people's minds worked. But this one's a classic.' He passed over another picture, this time of a woman in full queenly regalia, interrupting what was obviously a very vigorous blow job to announce, 'Who said anything about eating cake?'

'Marie Antoinette?' I asked.

Ray nodded. 'The sad thing is, a lot of people today simply wouldn't get the joke; not because it isn't funny any more, but because they don't even know who Marie Antoinette was.'

'Are all of these worth that kind of money?' I asked, gesturing around the room.

'The originals are. But we don't display many of those; in fact, we don't even keep them on the premises. Security reasons, insurance purposes, and plain old preservation. Some of these photos are more than a hundred, even a hundred and fifty years old now; you can barely even look at them without them crumbling, let alone handle them. So we make digital copies of every photograph that comes in, to show clients, to lend to publishers, whatever. And they're also handy for reference. You'd be surprised how many forgeries come in these days, and more every year.'

'You mean, people dress themselves up as Edwardian priests, take a few photos and then try to pawn them off as the real thing?'

'The amateurs do. But there are also people out there who probably make a better living than I do, selling blatant fakes to the gullible. And I mean, blatant.' He pulled out a ring binder and, as if he could barely stand to touch it for any longer than was necessary, he dropped it onto the desk.

'The first few pages are ones we shoot in the studio here, for reference and, occasionally, to complete sets where there's a scene or two missing. If you look closely, you'll see a towel with the gallery logo placed unobtrusively somewhere in clear view, to identify the piece as one of ours. Otherwise, they're as close to how the original might have looked as we can get it. But the rest are ones that I've picked up over the years, including a few that had me fooled for a while.'

I opened the binder and, quite honestly, I had no idea what I was looking at. Beyond what was obviously there, of course. I passed over the ones Ray had just detailed, to the page after page of supposed fakes. 'OK ...' I began. 'So what makes these any different?'

Ray leaned over me, close enough that I could feel his body heat through our clothing. Although I doubted whether the photographs had anywhere near the effect on him that they were having on me. After all, if you spend forty hours a week surrounded by every sexual act and position you could imagine, you had to develop some kind of immunity.

'This one. The costuming is spot on, the furniture's more or less right for the period. But you tell me. Did late-Victorian servants really wear studs through their tongues?' I looked closely and, sure enough, denting the glans of a cock in mid-lick, a honking great piece of hardware. He pointed at another. Again, the clothes looked correct, the furniture seemed old. 'And that's the point. The furniture does look old today. But in nineteen-oh-whenever, it probably wouldn't have been brand new, but it wouldn't look like it had just come out of an antique mall, either.'

And so on. I soon spotted a nineteenth-century nurse being fucked by a 'patient' whose cell phone still lay on the bed alongside her; a milkmaid blowing a stable boy beneath a sky that was streaked by a jet aircraft's contrail; and, my favourite, a scene that even Ray admitted was perfect in every detail bar one. A door had opened behind the couple, and you could just catch the reflection of a flickering TV screen through the gap.

He continued his impromptu lecture. 'Sometimes it's the language that gives a picture away. There'll be a word in the caption that wasn't in use at the time the picture was meant to have been taken. It's surprising how many words for cocks and quims we've come up with in the last fifty years or so. The problem is, I'm trained to look for things like that, and we have the necessary equipment to scrutinise every picture that comes in. A lot of people, though, it never dawns on them, just as it never occurred to you, that such things can be faked. So they start their collections, they spend a small fortune and then one day they need to have it appraised.' His voice trailed off. 'It's got to the point where my firm doesn't even offer to value collections any more, unless we're actually being offered it for sale. That way, if we think there's anything amiss, we can just decline to buy and not have to give a reason. You know how they say a fool and his money are easily parted? Well, a fool and his temper come in a close second.'

'And a maiden and her virtue?' I smiled and, having checked that his office door was closed, reached between his legs to squeeze his balls. The men and women in his photographs are probably all stone dead cold now. But looking at them was making me hot all the same, especially with Helen's last-night experience still bouncing around my brain. Even as I looked through the pictures, losing myself in some remarkable feats, the back of my mind continued conjuring up a scenario: she's in bed, already tucked up, reading a magazine; she barely glances up as Terry steps in from the shower, crosses the room. And suddenly he's straddling her chest, pushing his erection into her mouth. Was she shocked, was she frightened, was she horrified? Or did she realise that he wasn't as oblivious to the state of their marriage as she thought, and decide to let him know that the feeling was mutual?

I remembered the pleasure in her voice; pictured the joy in her eyes as she sucked his cock; saw that same joy echoed in the eyes of the women (and men) in the photographs spread out before me. The laughing brunette

136

with a cock in each hand; the nun with one in each hole. And some of the most beautiful one-on-ones I've ever seen, a succession of girls who genuinely look like they're enjoying themselves (a far cry from some of the sour-pussed visages you see in modern porn), and real girls too. Not a silicone boob or collagen lip in sight. 'Look at this one.' A photo of a girl in the obvious throes of orgasm caught my eye and I pulled it across the table. 'She looks exactly how I want to feel.'

Ray ruffled my hair playfully. 'Well, I suppose I could be in conference.' He grinned broadly and clicked the intercom on. 'No calls for the time being, Janis,' he told the secretary who answered, then turned to me. 'One thing, though. I don't suppose you have any condoms on you?'

I kissed him. 'You don't need a condom for what I have in mind,' I told him and, trailing my hand down his abdomen, I sank to my knees before him and unzipped his fly.

***

I held him still hardening in my hand, and drew the hot weight towards my lips, swirling my tongue across his glans in long, soft, deliberate swoops. I felt him stiffen beneath my administrations, as I brought my lips, too, into play. His scent was strong; his taste was tart. I wondered if Ray had forgotten his shower this morning, but it didn't matter. The heat of his hard-on packed a flavour all of its own and I could already sense it building.

My mouth enclosed him, sucking gently as I drew him in. I held his cock at its very base, the palm of one hand cradling his balls, the other scraping long nails hard against his stomach beneath his shirt. I knew he was close; his breath was coming in sharp gasps, his muscles were tensing beneath my fingertips. I gave him one more long, loving lick and then pulled away.

'Do you have a camera handy?'

He looked down at me and arched his eyebrows. 'What, like a digital?'

'No. I was thinking of something older.'

Realisation dawned on his face. 'We'd have to go through to the studio.' He glanced at the day-planner on his desk. 'It's free all afternoon.'

I folded his erection back into his pants. 'Well, maybe we should drop in. I must say, I'm feeling just a little Victorian right now.'

'We'd better have a look in the wardrobe as well, then.' Ray took my hand and led me back across the main showroom and into a smaller room at the rear of the building, laughing as he heard me gasp. It was like stepping out of a time machine into the perfect replica of an early twentieth-century living room. Or, at least, what I would imagine one looked like.

'We had a shoot in here last night. A sort of *what the butler didn't see* series of him going about his business while the lady of the house flashes her bits behind his back.' He pulled out the storyboard. In one, the butler's asking if he should 'decant' the port; behind him, she has a bottle pushed up inside her vagina, and replies, 'No, I think I can get it out myself.' In another, the misguided servant is holding the cat up to the window and asking if the pussy can see the tits. The lady is on her back with her legs in the air, her breasts and cunt parallel. 'Yes, and the tits can see the pussy, too,' she replies.

And so on. I lay the cards on the table and, while Ray started fiddling with the camera, setting up the automatic function that would capture every frame of the action, I went to the wardrobe and began selecting my costume.

Nothing fancy, nothing posh. I would be a scullery maid, a scruffy little urchin in a tattered slip, the white bow in my hair my only concession to feminine beauty; Ray would be the head of the household, come to admonish me for neglecting my duties, for pouting around the house, for generally behaving like 'a week of wet Wednesdays'. And, adopting a fierce, New England cut-glass accent, he slipped into the role beautifully. So beautifully that, with a sharp pang of jealousy, I wondered just how often he had played it? That's another thing about these old photographs: though you invariably see the woman's face, the man's is either disguised, obscured, or absent altogether.

It wasn't a pleasant thought or feeling. Neither Ray nor I had ever discussed fidelity, it's just one of those unspoken conditions that you naturally assume you both agree to. And would it even count as infidelity, if he were the star of his own dirty pictures? Wasn't it simply a part of his job? Open the office, answer some emails, check the post, get his dick sucked, make a few calls.

I tried to push the thoughts out of my mind, but Ray noticed anyway. 'Hey, you OK over there?'

I nodded. 'Yeah, fine.' I leaned back on the bed.

'We don't have to do this, you know,' he assured me, as though it had been his idea.

I shook my head. 'No, I want to.' Actually, I didn't want to, but I wasn't going to back out now. If not for my own sake, then for that of the eager cock that flag-poled through his shirt tails.

He stood watching me for a moment, and I saw the first camera flash go off. 'Come on, what's the problem?'

'Nothing!' I spoke a little more harshly than I intended, raising my face to look him in the eye. It suddenly occurred to me that I'd been staring down at my hands. 'I was just ...' I was going to say 'I was just getting into my role,' but I was speaking too slowly, or he moved too quickly. But suddenly he was astride me and, even as my lips parted to form a word, they found themselves forming another shape entirely, a wide O, as his prick pushed in, past my teeth, over my tongue, thick and hot and thrusting. 'And you can keep sucking on it,' he half-murmured, half-growled, 'until you decide to tell me what the matter is.'

My heart pounded. The same thought, the same action, the same *re*action that had been heating my pussy all afternoon. Instinctively, without even being aware of the fact, I was sucking on him, drawing him deeper into my mouth, feeling the blood pounding into my lips to make them fuller, softer, a smoother ride for his slow, but so forceful thrusts. Flash! Flash! Even through my closed eyelids I could see the bright explosions of the camera, each one blending with the sensations of light that slashed through my head as his cock tip drove deeper, banging against the back of my throat.

The thought skidded across my mind: what if I wanted to speak, to tell him what the matter was? How could I with this monster pounding into my face? But why would I want to? Why would I ever want this to stop?

Flash! Saliva flooded from my mouth, squirming past his tool to run down my chin and drip onto my chest. I tried to slurp it back in, but the action only drew Ray even deeper, until his thrusts ended only when my face itself was pressed against his abdomen. He held me there, pushing my nose tight into his belly, my chin into his balls, as I wriggled my jaw and thrust out my bottom lip, to send new sensations rippling through his flesh.

Flash! Again I felt him tense, again, a tingling of that sixth sense that all women possess. The lucky ones, anyway, as a come-drunk girlfriend once reminded me. His moment was upon us. Flash! I broke his grip and pulled back, kept him tight in my mouth, but not so deep that his load was going to slip straight down my throat. Instead, I caught it, held it, swilled it onto my tongue, and then leaned towards the camera with my mouth wide open. Flash! Then I swallowed.

Ray leaned back, breathing heavily, his eyes still half closed. 'Wow, you really had me fooled there,' he whispered. 'You looked furious, and even after you said you wanted us to do this, I wasn't sure if I still did. You looked like you'd rather bite it off than suck it.'

'It was nothing,' I lied. I snuggled into his arms, pulling the bow out of my hair as I did so. And then, as if the thought had suddenly occurred to me, 'So why do you always cut your own head off when you take photos?'

'Me?' He laughed. 'I've never … you think … is that why?' He squeezed my shoulders. 'Oh Chrissie, I run the gallery, I don't star in it. I can honestly say this whole thing –' and he gestured towards the camera '– is as new for me as it is for you. We have models that do the fun stuff and, to be frank, they're welcome to it. I have a difficult enough time staying hard for as long as I do.

The idea of keeping it up all day ...' He shook his head. 'And all the posing! They'd need a zoom lens to find my cock if I had to do this on a regular basis.'

I cuddled closer. 'I dunno, you didn't do so badly. When will the pictures be developed?'

'I should have them in a couple of hours.' He swung his legs off the bed. 'Look, some of us really do need to get some work done this afternoon. So –' he reassumed his stern Victorian butler persona '– can I now assume that there won't be any repetition of your dour behaviour?'

I nodded sweetly. 'No, sir. I mean, yes, sir. I mean, sorry, sir. But, hey, I do have a question for you. When you did decide to risk it ... carrying on with our photos, that is, what made you choose *that* particular option?'

'Seriously?'

'Yes, seriously.'

'I learned long ago there's this prejudice in society that blow jobs are somehow the guy's way of asserting some form of dominance over a woman, that she's not demeaning herself by doing it, but expressing her submission. I've never believed that. I think it's the guy who's being the submissive; it's like a cat or dog rolling over and showing its tummy when it wants to prove it's not a threat. There's sharp teeth in there, a mouth can do a lot of damage to a dick. So any guys who offers himself to be sucked is actually offering more of himself – trust, faith, love – than I think even he's aware of.'

143

I looked at him. Again, Helen and Terry came to mind and, in their case, that last word made sense. But Ray and I? 'Love?' I echoed.

'Well, yes. Plus, it feels so good that it's worth taking the chance. Oh, and by the way, that last photograph.' He stuck out his tongue in imitation of my pose. 'I have a client in Japan who'd pay me a small fortune for that, if he thought it was genuine. So if you do ever think about biting my prick off, just remember. You'll be the one who's paying to have it sewn back on.'

Hidden Inside
Ashley Hind

Sometimes when I see you I can't even breathe. I feel the air sticking in my throat and it never quite manages to escape before my chest flutters and sucks it back down. As the joy and adrenalin rush to build, the flutter becomes a kind of spasm, which perpetuates as I fail to draw another breath. I am left wondering if my self-preservation mechanism will ever kick in and force my lungs back into action. Fortunately, it always has, which is just as well as it would be a pitiful way to die: goggle-eyed and choking on an empty goldfish-gulp for oxygen, my big tits jiggling up and down and me looking for all the world like I have a cattle-prod stuck up my backside. The whole office would get to witness my graceless descent into a besotted heap at your feet, all watching

145

me struggle for one last longing look at you before my lights finally went out …

You probably wouldn't even bat an eyelid. You would be thinking: What is this very plain and slightly chubby (if sweetly perfumed) heap of nonsense doing wheezing and turning blue? Why is she spluttering saliva all over my very sexy Italian shoes? Too bad: I will die and never get to tell you that you are the most beautiful man that I have ever seen. You will never learn that, despite my relative plainness alongside others that you favour, I am quietly gifted in ways that would literally blow your socks off. I am, as it happens, the very best cock-sucker in … well, if not the whole world then at least in this office. And that, my lovely man-who-apparently-loves-to-be-fellated, is no idle boast but a fact.

If I was Hannah then you would have found out about my talent by now, that's for sure. But I am not her. All I am is a face that you recognise though hardly register. I know so much about you and yet nothing of me dents your conscious thoughts. To you I am merely a barely acknowledged shape that used to accompany Hannah to the staff canteen or to the pub, a splodge in your periphery as you filled your vision with her. I was the one who sat there silently while you two giggled at each other's sugges-tive remarks and nudged each other, shoulder to shoulder, in the only contact you would allow yourself in public. In private it is a different matter I'm sure. Despite

Hannah's claim that there is nothing between you but friendship, there is no way you would keep your hands off her if you got her alone. She is simply too gorgeous and irresistible and I would eat her up myself given half the chance. You remember that night you went to the cinema with her? You remember the other person, the one you steadfastly ignored in the bar afterwards, the one who had to sit with your best friend and not blurt out that he had a haircut like a fuzzy dog's arse and a terrible line in *Steven Seagal: Lawman* anecdotes? That was me! And I saw your face as you gazed upon her and I know it spoke of more than mere friendship.

* * *

It's the way my tongue flickers, or so I'm told. That's the secret of my penis-blowing gift. I can waggle the tip at a blurring speed and keep this up for ages. I have a good grip too, apparently. Somehow I innately know how hard and exactly where along each shaft to grasp, and precisely how fast to wank it at any given time during my performance. I don't know how or why I am blessed with such knowledge, I just am. I take a good hold and flicker my tongue with leg-shaking titillation at the very tip of the penis, giving it a teasing, wet butterfly kiss that goes on and on. Then I engulf the whole head (ensuring my mouth is full of saliva) and I suck – neither too hard, which might hurt, nor too soft, which just torments. I always do it just right. As I suck, I glide my hand swiftly up and down the shaft, urging the spunk from its hairy hidey-hole. As the lucky recipient starts to breathe harder and faster, I'm off again with my tongue, teasing some more but allowing his danger moment to recede. I keep this up for as long as he can, knowing each time I stop sucking that the sperm will not retreat as far as before, so it gradually builds and builds until it blows uncontrollably. I also know that, while my flickering tongue is exquisite, the real joy comes from having this tease interrupted by the warm bath of my mouth wrapping around his straining glans, and the bliss of my hand flashing up and down at such a rate on his hard shaft. It is all about timing: knowing when to lap and when to suck, about doing it exactly as he would beg you to do it.

And I will drink his spunk too, all of it, no matter how much. It's not that I like the taste, it's just that the whole rudeness of it turns me on. Not like our Hannah, eh? She screws her face up and spits it out like it was poison, like it was some hideous gloopy, acrid concoction tinged with salt and last night's curry, rather than the purest demonstration of your lust for her. You give her that reward and she nearly vomits on it. What a disappointing way to end such a vulgar but intense act – and you should know! I know because I have seen her do it. In fact it was she who first declared me such a blow-job expert. I never thought I was doing anything out of the ordinary. I sucked cocks in a way that I liked and drank the come like I thought I was supposed to. The boys seemed to like it but then they would say anything to get you back on your knees behind the hedges to drain their balls. The guys I got to blow weren't A-listers like Hannah's conquests and they were glad to get any female attention (I believe there is a phrase about not looking or fucking a gift horse in the mouth, or something like that). Anyway, it was Hannah herself that told me I did it so well. I shocked her into admitting that, to use her very words, I did it so much better than her.

'Christ! You kept that quiet, didn't you?' she spluttered some time afterwards, still unable to believe the extent of my prowess.

She looked at me for ages, gazing into my eyes, trying to fathom me. In the end, she just shook her head and shrugged.

'Everything about you is hidden inside,' she said. 'Why won't you ever let people see?'

She was wrong. It is not hidden. It is all there if only you would look for it. But with me, no one is ever looking. She should have known this more than anyone. If she gave me more than just a cursory glance then she would have realised that I was besotted by her.

***

It pains me that you know nothing about my life. I have a little catalogue of stored thoughts about you. I have snippets that I glean from any source possible to build up a picture of your ways and habits. I keep them in my brain in a file marked 'Infatuation'. I know it sounds a bit spooky but don't get freaked out! I am no stalker. I'm just lost in you and can't help myself. Do you know how agonising it is to want someone and yet fail to even register on their radar? That's when I hate 'Love': when it hits you with its full force, slams into you and seeps into your cells, burns your heart and flips your stomach with its conniving chemicals that turn you to mush. Love shouldn't be able to touch you unless your target's feelings are reciprocal. However, in Nature's cruellest twist, it will so often hit you doubly hard when you are open and vulnerable like this. It almost stands to reason that the apple of your eye will love someone else instead, and I guess it is life's final dagger to the heart to ensure that that someone turns out to be your own best friend.

Do you know I have been Hannah's best friend for twelve years – nearly half my life? No, of course you don't. Do you know that she was the first girl I kissed, the first girl to suck my tits? Has she told you that we used to masturbate in my bedroom? Or that one time, as we were both about to come, she scissored me and squashed our little pussy lips together in the warmest, wettest, most sublime kiss that I have ever had? I still think that was my most intense orgasm to date – or maybe it was the one straight after, when she silently watched me frig frantically with the thoughts and feeling of what she had just done to me fresh in my mind. I can never quite attain the same intensity now, although the memory is only a little fuzzy at the edges.

I recall the episode so often when I am alone with my hand between my legs, wishing she had let something happen between us again. Nothing ever did, though. We still masturbated together a few more times but as she approached her climax she would turn away from me. The second time she did this I left my own pussy alone, shuffled across to her and slid one wet finger up her bum to help her on her way. I bet she never told you this as you were worming your way up inside her pretty little bottom? She came very hard but never said a word to me after. I did it to her again the next time and I'm sure she pushed her bottom out for me. She left me straight afterwards, without saying much. I actually needed her to go. Once she couldn't see me, I fucked myself like mad, the finger that had been inside her squashed under my nose. Even worse, when I was about to come I put that same finger right in my mouth and sucked it! Actually, maybe that was the most intense orgasm I have ever had.

We never masturbated together again. If I suggested it, she would just shrug and say that she didn't feel like it. She just bounced off the bed to leave me all alone and torn in two. I loved her long before she stopped our wanking sessions, but the agony of her refusal to let me touch her just cemented my infatuation. I have wanted her more than anyone ever since – until you, of course. I was desperate to be in her bum again, to kiss her, to lick her lovely pussy. What tortures me most is the new-found knowledge that I am also one of the best exponents of cunnilingus on earth and that if I ever had or could give her just one sample of my gift then I am sure she would want more and make me hers forever. All I ever seem to need is one go with my tongue on the right people, and all my dreams would come true! It's mad, isn't it? I could make you fall in love with me if you could just see through my plainness and let me do the most personal thing to you that you could imagine! It's a shame my skills are not transferred some other, less illicit way – through a handshake, for instance. Perhaps I should become a Freemason.

* * *

We are all the same with the lights out is a saying, but it isn't true. With the lights on I am almost invisible. I'm the less attractive one of the pair or group, the one who doesn't say much but is actually quite sweet and funny if you gave her the time of day. Turn the lights off and I don't just become an equal. I soar above all. I leave the others stranded in a heap of mediocrity as my tongue plays its heavenly tune upon you. If you don't turn the lights back on your imagination need never fade. I'm not ugly, not by any means. I just don't shine as brightly as others and that makes me irrelevant to most eyes. I should stick to the dark, and I'm not talking about the gloomy corners of nightclubs where romance is snuffed out and leering drunks slur their desire to fuck you up your sexy fat arse. I should be an owl, or a vampire perhaps (which, come to think of it, is actually much sexier than something that hoots in trees and turns its head backwards). All this would be lost on you though, because you are a creature of the light, someone to be seen and adored, illuminated by the sunlight just like you were today, when I saw you and had one of my can't breathe/eyes googly/ please take that electrode out of my backside moments.

You were standing at the open window behind your desk, one arm up resting on the frame. It was so hot but as always you wore one of your smart shirts with the cufflinks. The cotton clung to you but it still seemed fresh and immaculate, and there was only one faint trace of sweat in the drops soaking little darker spots around your ribs. The light was shining right through the material and I could see the outline of your arm and the definition of your muscles. I could see the flaring behind your armpit, that little wing that connects the limb to the body below the shoulder (in most men unnoticeable but in you so proud and taut). This particular muscle is called the latissimus dorsi. I know this because I have looked it up. You would know its name because you have worked on it, sweating pints as you repeated the particular exercise that would increase its size and power, just as you have done with every muscle in your body. The beauty is that you could never be described as a 'bodybuilder'. Your brawn doesn't bulge narcissistically from your clothes and your sinew doesn't strain at your neck. No, you are just right. You are powerful and firm without being inflated or ridiculous.

I know you work hard at perfecting your shape. I know that you need to exercise without fail on a daily basis and that as soon as you get home you go into your garage to pump some iron, kissing your wife before disappearing for three-quarters of an hour while she makes your tea. I know that you then shower and come down, kiss her again and devote the rest of the evening to her and your two young children. I assume she is more than happy to lose you for this short time and why in heaven's name wouldn't she be? In fact, I know she is happy because while you are busy making yourself look even more wonderful, she not only makes your tea but hangs your suit up, gives your shoes a quick shine before tidying them away, and then unpacks your briefcase and washes out your plastic lunchbox, ready for the next day. Such devotion! Presumably she then gazes lovingly upon you and wishes away the hours until you come naked to her, your beautiful prick sticking out hard towards her. You will let her cuff your hands behind your back, shelving your machismo in your desire to be at the complete mercy of an adoring mouth and tongue. Because that's what you like more than anything, isn't it? More than fucking even, you love to be sucked dry.

Of course it was Hannah who told me all this, because she tells me everything. You regale her with tales of your secrets and she passes them all on to me! Strange then that she should lie about the fact that nothing sexual has actually happened between the two of you. According to her, you told her about your infatuation with all things blow-jobby one evening when you were a little tiddly and frisky. Perhaps you thought it might encourage her to have a quick go on your stiffy, although she claims, as she always does, that she just laughed it off. Rubbish! She sucked you off and probably more besides – I'm absolutely sure of it! Why she lies I do not know. It certainly isn't to spare my pain; she has no idea of my feelings towards you and is far too busy looking your way to witness my pathetic doting face. And you, you are too busy doing your puppy-dog expression right back at her to notice me at all.

***

Sometimes it rips me to pieces to watch the two of you together. There is such poetry between people who are desperately attracted to one another. There is a body language that shouts their need even if the face is pretending like mad that nothing out of the ordinary is occurring. There is a correspondence of speech and looks and laughter that has been automatically tailored in those moments together. It is an assimilation of each other's character that occurs from the very start, so that you do not offend or repel what you most want to grab hold of. It then forms and evolves. You create your own special traits between you that define your private moments and convince you that you were made for each other, even if you are actually married to someone else and have produced two children. And then everything you tell her she promptly relays to me. She talks about you as if it's just idle chit-chat, mere office observations. But I know that when you really like someone all you want to do is talk about them, to say their name out loud because the simple hearing of it is so exhilarating. I should hate her for spouting on eternally about you but perversely I do not. She is my window on your world and the fact that she knows your every privacy allows me to know you too. I will settle for any scraps I can get, even if the manner of receiving them breaks my heart.

***

Hannah was never the same with me once she ceased our masturbation sessions. She still loved me, but more like a younger sister than a girlfriend. She saw me as some kind of pitiable sidekick that needed looking after. She spoke up for me, made my decisions and ensured that I did not get overlooked by boys. In essence, this meant that when she went out with some handsome hunk, I got to go out with one of his less attractive friends, often the ones with a face like a pizza dropped onto the kitchen floor. Once I was even honoured with one of her own conquests. It was my nineteenth birthday and my so-called boyfriend had dumped me rather than buy me a present. Hannah had been seeing some lanky floppy-blond Irish chap called Rory for a week or so and had spent most of that time delightedly telling me how long his cock was. I was forlornly dragging around after the both of them and so, rather than palming me off on another of his friends, she bestowed me with the dubious gift of letting me stick around gooseberry-fashion while the two of them made out. She suddenly got a surge of impishness and whipped out his long prick. Giggling away, she then proceeded to get to her knees and suck him. When she came up for air, she was taken by a sudden moment of generosity. Remembering that it was my birthday after all, she offered me a go on this most delectable of lengths.

157

'You don't mind do you, Rory?' she asked, just in case he didn't want someone as plain as me gobbling away on his tool. Indeed, no – Irish raver Rory didn't mind at all, at all. In fact, he minded even less once I had got down and commenced my routine. He liked it very much, actually. I could feel her stiffening beside me, the first time I had felt anything like jealousy coming off her, although at that stage I didn't know why she should feel such a thing. Rory was quite obviously having the time of his life, gasping and panting away, so much so that Hannah decided it was time to ease me aside and get back into action herself. But Rory was more than a little disappointed by her efforts and, would you believe it, he held her still and jovially requested that I be given another go! Well, it was my birthday, so back into action I came, although I sensed Hannah was less happy to oblige me this time. She stayed silent as I went back to teasing her boyfriend and making his eyes screw tight shut, wringing from him the yelps and sighs that she could not.

She couldn't bear to force her way back onto him and suffer another embarrassment of being second best, so she staved off her jealousy until the point of no return. She elbowed me aside just as young Rory was ready to pop, sinking her mouth onto him to steal the glory, only to remember way too late that she had no stomach for spunk. I allowed myself a sly smile as she spluttered on his bubbling seed and then retched it back out onto his balls and belly. My private smugness did me no good. I have never had the chance to shout to the world that in one way at least I am better than her. I have kept this knowledge hidden inside. I never advertised my talent and neither did she on my behalf. After that, she stopped looking out for me as she once did. She gave her begrudging verdict of my skills afterwards and opened my eyes to the fact that I was genuinely and surprisingly expert at this dirty act, but she never shared her boyfriends with me again and all I got to blow on were her cast-offs and second-rate bastards who did not deserve or even understand me, let alone love me.

***

So I have been standing in her shadow all of these years, wanting her, wanting what and who she had. It's not about hiding my light under a bushel. It's simply about the crisis of confidence that prevents me from speaking out and being noticed. It's like this: you get noticed, they get to see how plain you are. A lack of self-belief renders you mute. It scrambles your senses and freezes your tongue. By the time you have thought of what you should say it is way, way too late. Every now and then, I get a surge of desperation and try to assert myself, try to seize the initiative. Earlier this year, with the two of us at a club and her staggeringly drunk after a fight and split with her boyfriend, I sat Hannah down and patiently explained to her how much I cared for her and needed her. I told her I wasn't gay but I loved her more than anything and couldn't think of anyone I would rather be with. I thought she understood me but when I tried to kiss her she suddenly came back to her senses and told me in no uncertain terms to fuck off and leave her alone, and to find somewhere else to stick my dirty lezzy tongue.

That 'somewhere else' found me, as it happened – abandoned outside the toilets, distraught and crying. It was a woman of maybe forty-five, brash and tarty, but too horny to let me escape her clutches once she had comforted me and I had told her what I'd done. And thus I shared another detached night with one of life's cast-offs, learning after a whole night of wet writhing that I was in fact as blessed in the pussy-licking department as I was at cock-sucking. That woman still calls me up now, unable to resist my talents and safe in the knowledge that I am too weak to refuse her. She summons me to her dingy flat to spank me hard and fill me with her fingers, and then to make me lick her pussy and her arse. This is my only experience of 'loving' another female, despite my longings for Hannah. All I can ever think of while my tongue is flicking over that fat pink clit and the juice is pouring out over my chin, are these same words: if I could just find a way to lick Hannah, I would surely make her mine.

Buoyed by the knowledge that I was the World Rug-Munching Champion, and by the fact that Hannah seemed to have no recollection of the nightclub incident, I made another play for her just recently. This time I shrewdly waited until she was equally drunk as before and twice as horny. I got as far as her room, got as far as seeing her lying on the bed, rubbing herself over her skimpy panties until they were soaked – I even got to see them coming off. I just caught the briefest glimpse of her shaven quim before she came to, saw me gawping at her and once more sent me packing in her foul-mouthed, aggressive-drunk way. I slunk off, sneaking her soiled panties with me as a prize to breathe in as I lay sobbing and frigging on her sofa. I know it's pathetic but you would understand if you loved her as desperately as I do. Or did, at any rate, because now, of course, all I can really think about is you. I'm not a bad person, I am quite the opposite. I am deep and sensitive, caring and funny. All I want is someone who can see past face value and search for the real me. All I want is someone beautiful for a change.

* * *

I guess it was obvious that you would fall for Hannah and never even see me. You must feel the waves of longing that radiate from me. I am conscious that they must fill the room they are so strong. Perhaps you mistakenly believe they are emitted by her. Maybe nothing of me features on your frequency. She should never have homed in on you, but she is such a flirt she simply couldn't help but reel you in. The fact that I have to stand by and watch the two of you basking in each other is what withers me most. I know if she had just opened up to me that one time then she would still be addicted to me now and would never let me go. I know that if she ever let me watch the two of you together, if just once more she deigned to allow me to drop to my knees and give my gift to her boyfriend, then you would choose me over her for ever. Victory is constantly dangled before me but I am always light years from grasping it. I tell you I am not a bad person. In fact, I am beautiful in so many ways, if for once people would just pause to allow a consideration of aesthetics. I didn't set out to destroy anyone and I'm still not quite sure of my reasons for doing it now. She says there is nothing between the two of you. Well, if she is telling the truth then innocent people are going to get very hurt. If she is right then you won't even recognise the offending item when your wife holds it before you, the tears already bursting from her eyes. You won't recognise the fabric or the scent that is still so faintly noticeable if you just press them to your nose and breathe them in deeply.

But Hannah is not telling the truth. I see the looks

between you, the indisputable signs of covert intimacy. The first time I witnessed it I was shocked to the core. The two people I most wanted and adored and suddenly there was this big secret between them, this telltale intense familiarity. I am used to having to wait in line but, you know, this time it hurt, it really did. It wasn't just a little bang but a bazooka shot to the heart, a crushing jolt that scattered my insides out. It just seemed like one too many defeats, one loss I could not absorb like all the others. So this morning I took my greatest treasure and gave them one last secret sniff in the washroom as I played with myself. I wanted to push them inside me but I didn't want to leave any clues. I went back out and watched you as you stood by the window, lit up by the sun and by everything that you are. Then, once you went out of the office, I snuck over to your desk and stuffed Hannah's stolen come-tainted knickers into your brief-case. And there they still are now, hidden inside your lunchbox where you won't find them, but your wife most certainly will, going about her loving evening rituals on your behalf, just as she does every night – right about now, in fact. Hearts are going to get ripped open and worlds are about to tumble down, but I'm just so fucking sick of coming last all the time. This time I get to make my statement, even if it is a silent one. This time I get to shine, and no one gets to stop me.

Grizz
Heather Towne

He was bent over picking up something, and his huge butt almost burst the seams of his tan shorts, his hairy legs glistening in the sun. I gripped the railing, staring. Then he straightened up, dropped the piece of trash into the canvas bag he had with him, and turned around. Giving me a good look at the guy, at his huge, hairful body. The zoo had never been so much fun.

I'd gotten a summer job driving seniors around on 'field trips', and today was the Sundowners trip to the zoo. Thirty men and women old enough to remember seeing dinosaurs in the wild, slowly making their way via wheelchairs, walkers and welded hips through the huge suburban animal oasis. Just me and a couple of female attendants to make sure the crowd of blue and

164

grey hairs didn't become part of a lion's breakfast, or get lost amidst the other cold-blooded creatures in the reptile house.

It was an OK job, and it would nicely pay my tuition for the next college term. So, I wasn't complaining, too much. Especially when I spotted that burly bear in the grizzly enclosure.

He was cleaning the den, right at home himself with his thick hairy arms and legs, shaggy head and barrel chest and bristling beard. His fur was brown, darker on his arms and legs, lighter on his head and chin, heavy all over. He even moved like a bear, lumbering around looking for stray garbage that had blown or been flung into the *Ursus arctos horribilis* habitat, and then loping after it, pawing it up off the ground.

'Wait 'til you see the polar bears. You'll really get a woody.'

That was Myron Dashowitz, from his motorised wheel-chair, staring at the bulge in my jeans that had arisen like salmon-back in a shallow stream. I glanced down at the old-timer. He looked up at me, waggling a pair of bushy white eyebrows that would've put Mark Twain to shame.

I grinned, blushing.

I was still brand new to the whole 'gay scene', not 'open' at all; unlike that grizzly bear playpen. But I'd quickly discovered that hair was where my care laired. Big, beefy men covered in rich, thick whorls, wearing their fur like cloaks of honour, unashamed of their bushy forearms and legs, the pelts on their chests and backs, the tufts that burst out of collars and cuffs, hairlines that plunged into deeper, denser parts unshown.

'Uh, can I borrow your binoculars for a second, Myron?'

'See for yourself,' he responded with a grin, handing me the field glasses. Then he directed the twin telescopes strapped to his face back down at my crotch again. 'Just be careful with that meat there – there're animals around, you know.' He laughed, coughed, choked. Zipped over to a water fountain.

I raised the binoculars to my bright-blue eyes and zeroed in on the bear on the range. The nametag on a pumped-up pec read GERALD, and, up close, I could count the brown follicles on his huge arms and legs, if I had a month or so. He looked to be around my young age, despite his far superior growth. My long, skinny white body and feeble red faux-hawk paled in comparison to his overall tan, build and hair. His eyes were amber, teeth white and even and sharp.

I watched the erotic nature show from close range for about a minute or so. Until Myron banged into the back of my legs with his arthritic knees, propelled by his chair and erratic sense of direction. 'I need the spyglasses back, kid,' he wheezed. 'There's some interesting wildlife about to bust loose over by the birdcages.'

I handed the binoculars back to the old guy and he zoomed in on Jaycey, one of the female attendants. She was bent over wiping the drool off Wilf Brimmer's grizzled chin, her huge bronze tits hanging down and almost out of her neon-red tank top.

'She's gonna need a mop,' Myron cracked, 'to sop up all of Wilf's drool.' He poured the cup of water he'd gotten from the fountain into his lap. Then cried, 'Oh, Jaycey!' motoring on over to the busty blonde. 'Clean up in aisle Dashowitz!'

I turned back to Gerald, ogled him bending deep and wide to pick up something white and triangular-shaped. I squinted. It looked almost like a guitar pick. Gerald studied it, flipped it over, then pocketed it.

His head came up, sniffing at the air. And he spotted me watching him from the elevated railing thirty yards away. His eyes narrowed and his nostrils flared, the big muscles on his body tensing, like he was getting ready to charge. On all twos, he looked quite capable of leaping the empty pool and scaling the concrete wall to the iron railing.

I backed away, slowly. Then turned and ran for the group of seniors parked at the neighbouring polar bear exhibit. The aged and infirm always got culled by marauding predators first, right?

***

Grizzly bear fangs were going for hundreds of dollars on the black market, according to my lunchtime research. Was that what Gerald had picked up and pocketed, perhaps for his own personal profit? I pondered the possibilities, as I gave vent to the rest of my pees in the Windemere Gallery men's room.

I'd just dropped a load of Grey Bristlers off at the art gallery, and now I had time to drop another load. I closed my eyes and let heavily haired Gerald fill my inner vision. He was in his natural habitat now – my bedroom – naked, his sun-blasted, fur-blessed body on full display. His cock poled out thick and hard from the wild bush at his loins, purple cap bulbing from smooth, tan foreskin.

I clutched my own clean-cut pink prick and stroked. And bucked, envisioning and feeling Gerald's warm paw on my dick, his strong, long, red tongue swimming into my mouth, his other furry arm wrapping me close.

I pulled on the surging length of cock, other hand sliding around to clench my tightened butt cheeks. 'Bear job,' I moaned, the man in my head dropping down to his knees and devouring my dick in his huge, hungry maw. Then sucking on it with quick, powerful tugs.

'Bear spray!' I bleated, fisting in a frenzy, fondling my stiffened nipples. My balls boiled and cock tingled with imminent explosion.

'Hey in there, I gotta use the john!' someone yelled, banging on the stall door. 'You kids get outta there!'

My eyes popped open and I gave my head a shake, then my cock, in frustration. I yanked my shorts and pants up, tucked and zipped.

'Hey, this is the handicapped john, son,' Sid Fenneman chastised me, as I unbolted the door and sheepishly stepped out. 'You should know better.'

The hunched-over octogenarian was clutching a brochure labelled *The Art of the Nude Model*, and his sweatpants exhibited more expansion than they'd seen in years. He gave me a knowing wink and elbowed me out of the way.

***

The zoo closed to the public at ten. But what I had in mind was strictly private. So, I loitered in the bushes by the owl cages until ten after ten, then snuck out into the moonlit clear, ignoring the 'Who? Who?' challenges of the big-eyed night birds.

The zoo was dark and deserted, full of the eerie cries of peacocks and howls of wolves, instead of the usual ear-grating cries and howls of little kids. I made tracks for the Bear Den, slipping through the double doors and into the stuccoed tunnel that led to the glass-enclosed polar bear dunk tank.

Just one of the huge white bears was floating on the surface of the dimly lit water, no crowd to perform for now. He dipped his head down and gave me a dark-eyed stare from behind the glass. As another bear in back suddenly roared, 'What are you doin' in here? Zoo's closed!'

I spun around and stared at Gerald. I'd hoped it was his job to clean off the glass after hours and, sure enough, he had a bottle of industrial-strength Windex in one huge hand, a roll of paper towels in the other. 'I-I was watching you this morning,' I admitted, trying to stay calm as a Great White Hunter holding an elephant gun. 'And I, uh, thought ... I'd hunt you up – for some answers.'

His eyes narrowed, nose twitching. He dropped the glass-cleaner and paper towels, tremendous muscles tightening up all over his big body. He could smell fear!

'I, um, saw you pick up that ... tooth. And ... and stick it in your pocket,' I gulped. My bear-baiting scheme was coming apart like a pawed-over garbage bag. 'And, uh, I thought we should, you know –'

He charged. I ran.

But he caught me, locking me in a bear hug and slamming me up against the thick glass wall of the polar bear pool. The floating bear dived down, attracted by the vibrations, another slipping into the water above.

Brown bear's strong arms squeezed the breath out of me, his hot, hard body pressing close. I gasped, 'I ... I only wanted to talk, Gerald!'

'They call me Grizz!' he hissed in my ear. 'And like hell you only wanted to talk!'

One crushing arm unbanded from my body, and Grizz dug around in the pocket of his shorts. He brought his hand back up, pressed a sharp, white, triangular object against my throat. 'This what got you all excited?' he growled.

I stared at the reflection of his rugged face in the glass, the two giant polar bears floating right in front of me, black noses pressing close. My bear trap had trapped me.

'Or was it this that got you all excited?' Grizz breathed hotly into my ear. He undulated his powerful hips, driving his swollen cock in between my thinly jeaned butt cheeks.

'Nothing but a bit of bone, from some meat,' he added, pulling the sharp object – which I believe he was then referring to – away from my neck.

'Uh!' I agreed.

He hooked his hand back around and grabbed on to my cock. Which in spite of the fright of its owner, had still filled the front of my pants, thanks to the bear's warm embrace. Grizz squeezed the pulsating appendage, his other arm still wrapped around my chest, thick, hair-tufted fingers now digging into the flimsy fabric of my T-shirt, probing and pinching my nipples. His heavy slab of cock sank in between my buttocks and started pumping. The polar bears pawed at the glass.

I was on fire with the heat of the hairy hunk so close, gripping and groping my cock and chest, frotting my bum. My face and body burned. It was a mauling I'd been truly after, and it was a mauling I was getting.

Grizz clutched and pumped. Then chewed, nuzzling my neck, nipping at my flesh. Sending shivers of sheer delight racing through me – to match the hot pulses of pleasure pounding along to my heartbeat, brought on by his busy hands and buried cock.

But then he suddenly spun me around, and we were bare face to furry face. He attacked my mouth, slamming his kisser into mine, our lips mashing together. I was banged back against the glass by the ferocity of his oral onslaught, hardly able to breathe with his huge, carnivorous mouth sealed over mine.

I fought back, flinging my arms around his big body, not playing dead, but alive. He gripped my shoulders and fed on my mouth, hot breath filling my head, hot body pressing so close, flooding my senses. I heard the scraping of actual bear claws on the glass behind me, above the roaring and pounding of blood all throughout my being.

Grizz roamed his tongue into my cracked-open mouth, and I welcomed it with my tongue. His heavy pink poker thrashed around the inside of my maw, bulging my cheeks and brushing my teeth. I somehow wrapped my own tongue around the writhing appendage and we swirled our slippery lickers together, sexually communicating in a guttural language common to both man and beast.

Grizz pulled his paws off my shoulders and planted them on either side of my burning red face, forcing my tongue right out of my mouth, pushing his with it. He quickly sealed his hungry lips around my protruding sticker, sucked on it.

I surged with joy, the ravenous creature feeding on my outstretched tongue now, sucking strong and long on it like it was an outthrust cock. He almost vacced it right out of my mouth, his eyes glaring into mine, palms piling up my cheeks, giving me an exhilarating preview of just what things would be like if he ever got around to mouthing my prick. And man-eater that he was, I knew that he would.

My cock was swelled up tall and wide and pulsating in my pants, squished against Grizz's throbbing erection by the force of his massive body. Anxious to be let loose, so the bear-guy could maul it with his hands and mouth, tame the wild he-passion in me that I'd been hiding too long.

But he had other ideas, first – for his own satisfaction. One sensual thing at a time. Or two things, if you count both of his nipples. Because that's what he showed me next, suddenly freeing my face and tongue and pulling back, ripping his shirt open, baring his hairy, hairy chest. Buttons were still pinging off the polar bear glass, as Grizz grabbed my hands and planted them on his mat, jerked my head forwards.

173

I tried to cup his huge, muscle-hewn pecs, my pale hands blazing amidst all that brown fur and even deeper brown skin. His hair was surprisingly soft, almost slick, and I slithered my fingers through it, clutching at the beef slabs of his chest. Before sticking my pink tongue out and burrowing it into the mass, worming through and touching a hard, jutting nipple.

Grizz shuddered like a bear hitting just the right bark spot with his butt, as I pressed my face right into his fur and sucked his nipple into my mouth. Along with a whole lot of hair. I tugged on the rigid nub, tripping my tongue over the tip; did the same to his other flared nipple, revelling in the rich, springy feel of his hair in my mouth and my hands.

Abruptly, he shoved me down to my knees, ripped his shorts open and down. His cock sprang out into my face, just as thick and heavy and huge as I'd feverishly imagined, and felt. He gripped my head and yanked my face forwards, up against his enormous meatbone.

Bears aren't known for their subtlety. Grizz had spotted his prey and captured it, and now he wanted me to do his bidding, no questions asked. Well, I could perform like the best dancing bear, minus the fur.

I grasped his cock at the bushy base and breathed deep of the musky, woodsy scent of the manimal, running my other hand up and down a hair-drenched leg, petting his coat. Then I stuck out my tongue and rimmed Grizz's swollen dick-cap. He grunted and jerked, claws biting into my scalp.

I swallowed his slit-wide hood and tugged on it, the chewy meat filling my mouth. And he thrust forwards, savagely jamming his dong right down my throat.

I gagged, spilling tears and snot. I was no bear-tamer when it came to cock-sucking skills, but that didn't matter to Grizz. He simply fucked my mouth, holding my head and pumping his hips, surging his cock back and forth between my lips. All I could do was cling to the hair on his muscled legs and hold on for the ride, trying not to choke to death, or get a too severe case of whiplash.

But my own animal instincts actually proved highly attuned, because as Grizz drove my mouth even harder, banging my head around on the end of his pistoning cock, I sensed his impending release (the salty taste of pre-come at the back of my throat was a tip-off). So, I valiantly wrenched my head back and disgorged Grizz's massive dong in a bear-spray of breath and saliva.

He instantly spun around, shoved his ass into my face. I grinned, open-mouthed, drooling saliva.

They were the biggest, hairiest specimens of male buttocks I'd ever feasted my eyes on: twin, heaping humps of thick tawny flesh covered in light-brown fur. I slammed my mouth shut and swallowed. Then I reached out with trembling hands and placed my own pasty paws on the huge, hirsute cheeks.

Grizz grunted, slapping his hands down on his knees and leaning forwards, sticking his ass out even further, banging me in the nose with his crack. I clamped my hands onto his buttocks and squeezed. The size and the strength and the denseness were incredible, the fur coating something to marvel at. My fingers could barely make a dent in the hairy flesh, the beast's back cheeks were so hard. I had to use my fingernails to make the impression I wanted.

'Eat my ass!' Grizz snarled.

I stared into his cavernous crack, willing up the courage. Then I stuck out my tongue, tentatively poked it in between his two mammoth buttocks. He reached around and grabbed on to the back of my head, jamming my face into his ass crack.

I tasted the hairy, sensitive skin of his butt cleavage. And then I licked it, gripping his cheeks with dampened palms and bobbing my head in between, wetting his crack and asshole with my tongue. His buttocks shuddered in my hands, hair straightening up on end a bit, as I shot out my tongue full length and swiped it up and down his crack, lapping his ass.

It was amazing, exhilarating – my tongue busting free in another man's butt for the very first time. And to start off in such a deep and dangerous cleft, grasping such giant, furry glutes! My head spun, nostrils flared to suck in the musky, loamy scent of the king of the zookeepers, tongue licking and licking and licking.

I tugged at his cheeks, splitting them wider apart. His butt hole winked at me, hairy as the rest of him, glistening with the moisture from my mouth. I went wild, lunging my tongue up against his puckered brown-eye and swirling it all around, rimming the bear. He jerked with feeling, and I beamed with the same, squeezing my tongue right up against his sex opening, seeking to burst inside.

Grizz reached back with both hands and slammed them down onto my hands on his ass, and tore his cheeks wide open. My tongue surged inside his butt. I speared deep, sticking his anus, filling the first two or three inches of his chute, packing his ass with my tongue. Then squirmed the wet, budded mouth-organ around right inside him.

Grizz straightened up with a grunt, closing his ass on me all too quickly. He turned around and grabbed on to my shoulders and jerked me to my feet. Then he tore my jeans open, shoved them and my shorts down, exposing my own vibrating need. He closed a warm, damp paw over my pulsating shaft and took a few rough pulls, almost ripping me out by the ginger roots.

We kissed, Frenched again. I'm sure he could taste his ass on my tongue, and he enjoyed the scent as much as I did. And now he wanted to get my scent. He lifted me up in his arms and spun me around, twirling me like a caught salmon in the paws of a hungry bear. Until I landed upside down with my legs on either side of his bushy head, my cock up against his bristly face, his cock pressing up against my happy face.

It was the hanging 69! Something I'd only fantasised about in front of my computer in the privacy of my own bedroom. The blood rushed to my head at one end, my other head at the other end. As Grizz consumed my needful cock in one gulp.

I full-body jerked in his arms. He was holding on tight just below my upturned buttocks, and I grabbed on to his waist to keep from fainting. My meat was locked up in the hot, wet cave of the carnivore's mouth, turning me inferno with delight. I clung to the hair of his big body and took his own bloated clubhead into my mouth.

Grizz sucked on my cock, moving his huge head back and forth, pulling with his devouring lips and mouth, bathing and cushioning with his broad tongue. I moaned around his knob, shimmering with sensation, the bear sucking long and hard and deep. I swallowed up more of his cock, sucked on it again, hanging from the brute's shoulders this time.

Then I bit into his dong, as he went even more animal on my genitals. Grizz disgorged my pulsating cock and sucked up my lust-tightened sac. He ate up my balls, tugged on them, slapped around the individual nuts with his tongue, stirring up the sperm inside to the boiling point. Before he spat that ultra-erogenous zone out and shovelled his tongue into my crack.

I wound my fingers into the hair on his muscled thighs, whole body quivering out of control in his arms. Grizz was giving me the ass-licking I'd given him, only ten times as fiercely and forcefully. He tilted my butt up and swabbed his tongue in between my trembling cheeks, power-licking my bum cleavage.

It felt wild and woolly, wonderful. I sucked on his cock halfway in my mouth, my head jerking up and away with every drag of the bear's furry tongue along my crack. He had a voracious appetite for ass, like everything else, was brutally skilled in the art of eating same.

It seemed to go on forever, and ended all too soon. Grizz spun me around again and set me back down on my feet, then turned me a hundred and eighty degrees and bent me over and shoved me up against the glass, instinctively knowing what we both really craved.

He lubed his cock, with bear grease, perhaps. I whimpered when his blunt fingers dug into my crack and rubbed me slick. Then cried out and rose up on my toes when Grizz squished his bulbous cap into my ring, and burst through. He rammed his rod deep into my over-matched chute, hair on his balls tickling up against my wildly tingling buttocks.

There were three polar bears floating in front of me now, eyeing me hungrily, jaws open and razor-sharp teeth showing, as Grizz dug his claws into my waist and plunged his cock into my ass. He brutally banged me

179

back and forth, pumping hard and fast and oh-so-deep, his hairy thighs smacking up against my baby's bottom-smooth buns. My hands squeaked sweet agony on the glass, my body and soul rocked to the sexual core by the bear's awesome anal assault.

'Fuck! Fuck! Fuck!' Grizz grunted in rhythm to his violent thrusting. His purview was penetration and pounding, not poetry and peanut butter and jelly sandwiches.

I pulled a hand off the glass and grabbed on to my flapping cock, the polar bears snapping at the water as my mitt plunged downwards. My dick was numb-hard, my ass blasted with white-hot feeling.

Grizz roared, 'Coming! Fuckin' coming!' He tossed his head back and thundered his hips, plundering my chute with reckless abandon.

The image of that ecstatic bear shimmered in the vibrating glass, the other watching, wide-eyed bears floating in behind. Grizz jerked, and blasted, spraying my ass full of his sizzling sperm, marking me as his own. Just as I shivered with blistering joy, startling the gathered polar bear clan by splashing the glass of their underwater enclosure with superheated jizz, over and over.

* * *

Grizz was busted three days and five reamings later. Attempting to illegally sell grizzly bear fangs on Chinese eBay. One of his female co-workers tipped off the wildlife authorities, and a judge sentenced him to six months in a steel cave.

I'll visit him in hibernation, for sure. I'll be bringing some raw meat with me, of course, because there's nothing more savage than a caged bear on conjugal visit day.

I can hardly wait.

THE SILVER CHAIN – PRIMULA BOND

Good things come to those who wait…

After a chance meeting one evening, mysterious entrepreneur Gustav Levi and photographer Serena Folkes agree to a very special contract.

Gustav will launch Serena's photographic career at his gallery, but only if Serena agrees to become his companion.

To mark their agreement, Gustav gives Serena a bracelet and silver chain which binds them physically and symbolically. A sign that Serena is under Gustav's power.

As their passionate relationship intensifies, the silver chain pulls them closer together. But will Gustav's past tear them apart?

A passionate, unforgettable erotic romance for fans of *50 Shades of Grey* and Sylvia Day's *Crossfire Trilogy*.

GAME – JUSTINE ELYOT

The stakes are high, the game is on.

In this sequel to Justine Elyot's bestselling *On Demand*, Sophie discovers a whole new world of daring sexual exploits.

Sophie's sexual tastes have always been a bit on the wild side – something her boyfriend Lloyd has always loved about her.

But Sophie gives Lloyd every part of her body except her heart. To win all of her, Lloyd challenges Sophie to live out her secret fantasies.

As the game intensifies, she experiments with all kinds of kinks and fetishes in a bid to understand what she really wants. But Lloyd feature in her final decision? Or will the ultimate risk he takes drive her away from him?

Find out more at www.mischiefbooks.com

POWER PLAY – CHARLOTTE STEIN

Now she's the boss, everything that once seemed forbidden is possible…

Meet Eleanor Harding, a woman who loves to be in control and who puts Anastasia Steele in the shade.

When Eleanor is promoted, she loses two very important things: the heated relationship she had with her boss, and control over her own desires.

She finds herself suddenly craving something very different – and office junior, Ben, seems like just the sort of man to fulfil her needs. He's willing to show her all of the things she's been missing – namely, what it's like to be the one in charge.

Now all Eleanor has to do is decide…is Ben calling the kinky shots, or is she?

Find out more at www.mischiefbooks.com

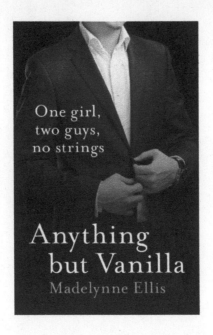

ANYTHING BUT VANILLA
MADELYNNE ELLIS

One girl, two guys, no strings.

Kara North is on the run. Fleeing from her controlling fiancé and a wedding she never wanted, she accepts the chance offer of refuge on Liddell Island, where she soon catches the eye of the island's owner, erotic photographer Ric Liddell.

But pleasure comes in more than one flavour when Zachary Blackwater, the charming ice-cream vendor also takes an interest, and wants more than just a tumble in the surf.

When Kara learns that the two men have been unlikely lovers for years, she becomes obsessed with the idea of a threesome.

Soon Kara is wondering how she ever considered committing herself to just one man.

Find out more at www.mischiefbooks.com

www.ingramcontent.com/pod-product-compliance
Ingram Content Group UK Ltd.
Pitfield, Milton Keynes, MK11 3LW, UK
UKHW022246180325
456436UK00001B/24